My name is Lang Vandervelt, but my friends call me Van. I became someone else, or should that be *something* else. And this is how it started. With Raph, my friend and teacher, I formed the Time Grafters. This starts the story of how we laid the foundations on which everything would be built. And when I say everything I mean both the good and the bad.

I0531581

# Order
### Foundations: Book One

## BY: PG SOMERSET

For Drew,
in the hope of discovering
new adventures

Published in 2015 by Whelkum Books, an imprint of Whelkum Productions.
Copyright © Whelkum 2015

# Other Time Grafters Books

**Running Out of Time** – Origins Book One
**Death at the Beginning** – Origins Book Two

## Coming Soon:
**Inside a Nightmare** – Foundations Book Two

# Time-Grafters

# Order

## Foundations: Book One

# **PROLOGUE**

It was in fact the actual planet Mars, but it looked like a model. The monster that stood looking at it was standing on nothing, and *that* nothing surrounded him. If the ghostly figure was actually in our universe he would have been more than 27,000 kilometres tall. The phantom drifted around the planet. Its face was incapable of emotion, and yet disapproval still managed to shine in its eyes.

Mars' Green Belt circumnavigated the whole of the planet's equator. The fission satellites, or human-created mini-suns, made the green band glow day and night. It stood out from the planet's red soil like a fungi grin.

The belt was made of plants brought from Earth, but they had evolved in their new environment. Mars' reduced gravity had changed them. They were taller than on Earth; their leaves were broader and the stems thinner.

"This is wrong," the monster declared.

Another entered the nothingness. They looked identical, twin nightmares with long, horse-like faces. "It is what they are making that is wrong."

"Are *they* wrong?" a third asked with dust-dry rasps. All three spoke with voices that sounded like they had not been used in a thousand years.

"They *could* be," said the first. All three had about them a deadness that nothing in this universe could possess.

One of the monsters leaned forward, looking at something near the planet. "If they are wrong, would we have to cast them out?"

"They go beyond Casting; they require Ordering. We will work backward from this moment and order existence without them. It is the only thing that would stop them from doing this again," the first one said, joining the other one whose attention was focused past Mars at a spaceship impossibly small when compared to the planet. It was a United Earth Consortium deep-space explorer-class ship. Its silhouette looked like a ring passing through a large cube. The fact that it resembled a doorknocker gave the ship's class its nickname: "Welcome Ships." The enormous nightmares glowered down at the ship with the most unwelcoming look they could express. "We are unanimous then: Earth and its spawn will receive Order."

# CALLING TIME OUT

It was the biggest room I'd ever seen. It was massively massive. A friend of mine named Smudge would have called it 'stupid big'. It was so big that it felt even bigger than it was. It felt like that feeling I get when I step off a step I didn't know was there. Do you know what I mean? I had the feeling of freefall, even though my feet were both on the floor. It was like that big, and I'd just stepped into it.

All I could do was look around. I was standing in front of the wooden kiosk with a yellow door that I'd just stepped out of. The kiosk looked like something you'd find at IKEA. It was wooden and curved away from me, a glass awning circling it like a halo. Its surface was super-glossy and its colour was a stained, dark orange. The normal-sized door I'd just stepped out of was curved too, and painted mustard yellow. It had a round window at the top and a long, narrow window running the rest of its height. I reached for the brass lion's head doorknob and pulled. Nothing happened. The thing was more than locked, it was sealed.

I walked around the odd booth; it was maybe four metres wide. It was totally round. When I took a step back from it I could see a lozenge-shaped clock with six hands sticking up from its flat roof. I tried looking in its six windows, but it was too dark inside to see anything.

I was in New York I figured. I had lived in the U.S. for five years and had gone to New York City a few times. This hall, or station, looked a lot like Grand

Central. I just don't remember it being *this* big. It was more like New York in the movies. The place was virtually silent. The only sound I could hear was the quiet ticking of the strange clock.

So maybe I've gone crazy. And if that sounds like an odd statement here are my reasons for making it. In this uber-weird place, a few things are way wrong. Example: I don't remember the roof looking like a massive solarium with see-through steel beams and the brightest stars I've ever seen, just outside. Also I don't think they keep overstuffed, leather sofas and old-fashioned, wooden desks in a terminal. I'm pretty sure I remember Grand Central having stone walls holding up the roof. In here there are pillars, and lots and lots of books. But the best example that something was funky was the obvious lack of people. If this is Grand Central, one of the major transportation hubs in the world, shouldn't there be more people? The kiosk was standing in the centre of the room. I could make out all six corners, but there was not a soul to be seen.

"Wait," I said to myself. "The room is rectangular. How can it have six corners?" I looked and counted again. "That's the proof, I've lost it."

I yelled, "Hey, anyone here?" I waited, and waited. There was no response. I started walking around and yelling. If there was no one here, no one would mind. If there was, well then maybe they'd work out they had company. "Hello, anybody here? *Hello!?*"

Someone did show up, and I changed my mind. I wasn't crazy, I was dead. Here's how I got to that answer: The person who showed up? I knew him, at least I was pretty sure I did. He looked just like a friend of my best friend. The guy died at the beginning of the summer, it was all over the school's social media. Smudge was a wreck all summer. So despite him looking like a camp councillor with a white polo shirt, blue shorts, and boat shoes, I figured he was an angel. I added the parts together: the feeling of falling, dead guy in white in front of me, and not where I was a few minutes ago, they summed up to--dead. But dead where? Was this heaven or hell?

Raph, the dead guy, and I had been classmates. We shared a friend, we'd hung out a few times. He should know me. If this was heaven or hell, shouldn't he be expecting me? Someone would have called ahead right? The thing is, he looked as confused as me. He just kept staring at me. We stood there for a long time. I was trying to figure out what was going on; maybe he was too. Finally he said, "Sorry, but who are you?"

"Lang?" Why was I saying it like it was the answer to a maths problem? "Vandervelt, but my friends call me...Lang."

"Well, *Lang*, you can't be here, so...how are you?" He had that sort of tone that headmasters have. I think he knew I was lying. Now there's a genius idea for you: lie to an angel. No one calls me Lang. He looked and sounded like he was used to people trying to lie to him. Maybe he was St. Peter. But why would he look like Raph? I mean Raph was cool and all, but I always thought he was a bit slow, and kind of a loser. I mean I felt bad when he died, but I didn't really know him that well. He was just this guy who never seemed like he fit in too well. Not that I am, or was, Mr. Uber-Popular. Just that Raph was even more of an outsider than me.

Maybe this was Raph after all. We'd had science with Mrs. Jones last year, and Raph had that kind of raspy voice. He always sounded like he was going hoarse. "Good thanks, a bit...ah...wowed. Am I dead?"

That was obviously not the answer he was expecting. "I mean, *how* are you here? How did you get here? The Library is nowhere, and no-when. It has no way in or out without someone, or me only, requesting one."

"I was crossing Lawrence one second, and the next I was here," I told this Raph look-alike. "I was thinking maybe, you know, I died?"

He ignored that. "That can't happen."

"What, me dying? I think it *can* happen."

Raph sighed and rolled his eyes. "You're not dead."

"*Really?* I kind of think I am. You're dead, and you're standing in front of me." Oh man, what if he's a ghost who doesn't know he's dead? That'd be messed.

"Okay let's try again: where are you from?" I told him and his eyes grew wide. "*Who* are you?"

"Lang Vandervelt," I said, and then asked, "Who are *you*, or do I just call you Dead Guy"

"I'm really not dead, my name is Raph."

I shook my head. "Can't be."

"I am. I'm alive."

"No," I said getting a little annoyed, "You can't be Raph. If you're not dead, you can't be him."

"Alright, let's not continue this any further. I know who I am. What I don't know is what you are."

"Confused," I said. "Just answer me straight--is this the afterlife?" Great! I'm stuck in a movie set-style station with a nut-job angel guy whose train obviously left without him, if you know what I mean. And what's that about not knowing *what* I am? This guy was really starting to get me ugly.

The Raph-like guy actually smiled. "No, you're not dead. I'm not dead. I just faked it a long time ago. Glad to hear it worked."

I began to relax. Until then I didn't know how much tension had built up in my shoulders. "Okay you can drop the drama. A long time ago? It was like two months ago, not '*a long time ago*'," I said like someone in a movie preview.

"For you. For me it was like...." He looked up at the stars and actually started counting on his fingers. When he looked back at me he finished his sentence. "Well, let's just say a lot longer."

"Dumb answer," I said with a laugh.

"Okay. Let's just get over this. Orientation," Raph started. He waved his hand above his head, and I half expected him to say 'ta-da', "*This* is the Library. it doesn't exist in your universe, but it houses it. The Library is just about infinitely large, and I'm its controller."

"You?" I laughed. "If you really are Raph. The same Raph Smudge knew, then you'd remember how thick you are at history. He used to tell me all the dumb things you'd say in Mr. Hans' class. There is like no way you're a librarian."

Raph looked at me with a very level stare. It was like he was trying to look through me. When he continued it was obvious he was ignoring my joke. "It is possible that you came in when I was on Earth last, but why would you show up now? I need to get you back home, because you can't be here."

Raph walked around me and over to a sort of cluster or clump of tables. All of them were wood and looked like the sort of desk you'd see in an old library. Nothing interesting there then, but when he started moving his hands, things happened. It looked like he was casting a spell, and the effect was the same. Images rose up from the desktops and just hung in the air. There was a sort of boom that passed through the room, and me. It was like a shockwave; I could feel it in my chest. I swear there was a ripple that went along with it. As his hands slowed there were pictures of my street but from all different times. They weren't like photos but more...real. I mean, sure things were moving inside them like some sort of Hogwarts' painting. That wasn't the crazy part; I mean everyone's watched TV. I can't really explain it, but it was like they were actually there. I mean they were real and yet flat. He touched one, and the other vanished. Then he pulled up these 3D graphs right out of the tabletop and started touching points on each one. Every time Raph touched one, the others would change.

"This is tricky," he told me. "I'm trying to place you very close to a null-point."

"What's a null-point?"

"It's a chrono-obsolescence, or point in time and space, that doesn't exist anymore. There are a lot of them out there. This one is a bit more tricky."

Typically I'm a pretty trusting person, but I didn't believe him. I'm not sure why. I think it's because the answer came too quickly. "Well I can always catch a bus if I need to."

Just then the light from above changed from 'normal' to red. I say normal, but the light was about as opposite from normal as anything could be. It wasn't light so much as the opposite of a shadow. It started out dark up at the ceiling, but by the time it reached us down on the floor it was as bright as daylight. And now it had turned as red as a rose.

"That's a sign, isn't it?" I asked.

Raph was moving from one table to another, checking graphs and swearing. Sometimes he was moving so fast it was like he was at one and then another in a second. I just tried to stay out of his way. There was another boom and the light went back to its standard sunlight colour.

"Okay. Think I got it," Raph said looking relieved. He started walking towards the kiosk that I'd first come out of.

"How near are we?" I yelled to him as he walked the long way between the tables and the Scandinavian-styled mushroom.

"Walking distance! Come on!" he called over his shoulder and easily pulled open the yellow door.

I jogged after him but stopped just this side of the door. Part of me was worried. What if I woke up once I went through the door? Part of me--a big part of me--didn't want to wake up. On the other hand, I had the feeling that if I didn't leave now, this place might not let me go again. Suddenly it felt really creepy. I stepped through the door after Raph. It was still daylight; that part he'd gotten right. Everything else was wrong.

# WRONG PLACE, WRONG TIME

On the other side of the door the air was thin and smelled of vegetation. It felt like someone had planted a jungle on top of a mountain. All I could see were green plants. Trying to look through them for Raph I called, "This is your idea of close? I think we're somewhere in South America."

"Yeah, or it *might* be a bit further," Raph called back. He was reading a book when I found him. He nodded his head, suggesting I look up.

"That's a lot more than *a bit*," I said, trying not to sound hysterical. "Raph, there are four suns up there!"

He shook his head. "No. The one to the left is the sun. The other three are some sort of satellites. I am guessing that they are here for heating."

"This is your idea of walking distance!" I yelled at the idiot who couldn't even land me on the right planet. I pulled out my phone and checked for signal. I know it's illogical, but it was just something to prove that it was all real. Something normal, and who knows, maybe I'd be lucky. I wasn't. Point-of-fact, it was dead. It wouldn't even turn on.

"Don't worry, *Lang*. I'll get you back."

I didn't believe him, but I hid my doubts by keeping my eyes on my phone as I pressed the power button over and over again. "I don't get it. I just charged this like an hour ago."

"Yeah, the Library's portals can do that some-times. I think it might have something to do with chonorelativity. You know, passing in and out of the electromagnetic spectrum. Just forget it, let's take a nose around. We might find something interesting. I mean, when was the last time you were on another planet?"

He said *interesting*, but I had the oddest feeling he meant *trouble*. We started walking through the plants, which were about twice as tall as me. Then we seemed to cross a line of some sort. Suddenly they were huge as trees and blocked out the sky. Raph lead us along between these 'trees' until, just like before, it all changed. Now the plants were only slightly above my head. They were planted much tighter, like a cornfield.

It was weird that some of them looked like things I'd seen back on Earth, just bigger. I should also say that the soil was like nothing on Earth. It puffed as we walked, like sand in water, but then fell like snow. Also it was really dark red.

"Is it always like this?" I asked.

"Meaning?"

"Is going to a different planet always like this?"

I think Raph was laughing, but the thin air changed our voices. "It's been so long since I've just gone to visit somewhere else that I've forgotten."

It sounded like he was either trying to sound cool or jaded. Maybe he was telling the truth about being as old as he said he was. It was going on a half an hour of exploring when we came across a large metal platform in a clearing. The open space was maybe six metres square while the round plate was about four metres wide. Its surface was shiny like a mirror and was raised up from the ground by about six centimetres. It was anchored with four clamps that were about ten centimetres tall, or the height of my hand. The mirrored surface slotted into the clamps about halfway up. On the top of each anchor was a pole with what looked like a mini-tablet mounted on top. Each tablet was about the size and shape of my mobile.

"What is it?" I asked as I walked around the platform.

"Something we shouldn't mess with," Raph said looking like he was about to ignore his own advice.

On the far side from where we entered the clearing was a slight ramp up onto the mirror. "Look."

"What?" Raph asked from where he was examining one of the anchors.

"There's a ramp. Like this thing was designed for wheelchair access," I said, walking slowly around to it.

"Or cargo. Just don't mess with it," he added as he pulled off a clamp's outer casing and reached inside the small panel.

"When you say, 'don't mess with it', is that like your way of saying you don't know?" I asked as I stepped up onto the mirror.

"Don't!" he yelled, jumping up, and reached out towards me. The world shifted and the light changed.

When my eyes refocused we were no longer in the green jungle. We were in a large, metal room. It looked like a hangar. Oddly shaped crates and containers were everywhere. So were people dressed in military uniforms. No one had noticed us--not yet.

"We need to reverse the process so we can get back," Raph whispered and slowly rolled down off the plate.

"If we do that, won't someone see us?" I said, daring to only move my eyes as I looked around.

I felt so very conspicuous. I was standing on top of a mirror, in the middle of a wide-open space. I felt like the ballerina my sister had inside her music box. It was like I was just waiting for people to notice something out of place. I whispered to Raph from the corner of my mouth, "Hurry up."

There was a fizzing sound and Raph swore under his breath. "What do you think I'm doing, knitting?"

"I think you're *not* hurrying up," I hissed trying to remain motionless. I was beginning to feel like a shop mannequin.

Just as I chanced a look down at Raph, someone did what I expected: she noticed us. "You there! Step away from the MaTeS!"

"Got it. That should do...it," Raph announced and jumped onto the mirror. Everything shifted again.

I was expecting to see the Christmas colours of the red and green planet. I was surprised to see nothing but grey, and then I remembered that Raph was driving. We were somewhere else. The only light was from an open door about ten metres away. It cast long shadows across the distance between it and us. Thanks to these low lighting conditions, it took me a few seconds to realize that we were not on a mirror platform.

"You suck," I said as I crouched down to where Raph was lying.

I looked around. The world had gone even further down the weirdness scale. I was somewhere like I'd never seen before. In this light the walls looked like they were made from grey tree bark. They weren't straight up and down but rounded and irregular. The floor felt slippery and squishy, like it was made out of old jelly. We were obviously way off course. "You need to get satnav."

"Or you could look at it as a chance to see more of the universe," Raph suggested as he, too, looked around.

There was one of those platforms about three metres to our left. It was the only thing that looked manmade in the room and looked totally out of place. "What are those things?"

Raph pulled out the same travel guide he'd been reading before and slowly started turning on the spot. The more he turned the more serious he started to look. "They're Matter-Transition Systems or Ma-Te-S."

"That's stupid. There's no 'E' in transition," I said looking at the platform and the cause of our troubles.

"Really? That's the part of 'moving matter at a rate faster than light' that you have a problem with?"

I blushed, he had a good point. "If they are matter-transmitters, then did we end up off it?"

"Good question." Whatever he was reading, he wasn't liking it.

"Here's another good one: why are you reading a book? What is it, 'All You Want to Know About the Universe But Are Ttoo Afraid to Ask'?"

Raph didn't bother to look up. Instead he shook his head. "No."

"Oh, then it's...?"

"It's part of the Library. You remember how I got us here?"

"Yeah. Badly." Raph glared at me and I took the hint. "Okay, yes. You did that desk *magic*."

"Magic,." Raph said as he flipped a few pages. "Interesting."

Instead of watching him read, I started looking around again. I didn't like the looks of this place. Suddenly being a human mannequin in a hangar full of soldiers was starting to look good compared to hiding out here. The air was so dry that it felt like dust in my mouth. "Do you know where we are?"

"No." His clipped answer should have told me more than it did.

I was starting to get annoyed again; this time by how much he was leaving me to guess. "Then how are you looking it up in a travel guide?"

"The Guide gathers information. It also translates and is an interface with the Library," Raph said finishing his revolution.

"You've been on your own for a long time, haven't you?" I asked.

"Very. Why?"

I stomped on his foot. In shock and surprise he looked up at me. "Because you've forgotten that there is more to life than books. Hello!" I waved, "Person here who would like some of that information, too. Let's start with, what happened?"

"Yeah okay, it's been a while, but still--ouch. You know that hurt, right?"

"That was sort of the idea. Let me put this in a way you might understand. W. H. E. R. E. space A. R. E. space W. E. space A. N. D. space H. O. W. space D. O.

space W. E. space G. E. T. space O. U. T. space O. F. space H. E. R. E. question mark."

"Now that's just rude," Raph said shaking his head. "Okay, as best it can tell, the Guide tells me that we're in a spaceship heading towards Mars."

"Rude, but effective," I insisted. "Mars?"

"I think that's where we were when we left the Library," he said, reaching out and touching the rough, wonky wall behind us.

"So then the answer to my second question is...?"

"*Hide,*" Raph hissed. Something was casting a long shadow across the room, but the shadow was shortening. Someone was coming. We ducked behind a low, panelled wall just to our right, and while Raph read his book, I poked my head around the corner. It wasn't someone, it was some*thing*. Its head looked like a hailstorm. Okay, if I said its head looked like the contents of a snow-globe, only with no glass, would that give you a better image?

The 'head' was disturbing enough, but what was below had me gagging. It had no clothing on, and nothing to hide. Its body was like a corpse doll, with only limp flesh hanging over and off a skeleton. Its feet shuffled, but it still moved faster than you'd think it could. As it entered the room and approached the platform its shape changed. It went from the worst-looking action figure ever into a uniformed human. By the time it vanished, there was no difference between it and any other helmeted soldier.

I pulled my head back around the corner. "What was that?"

"I don't know," Raph whispered.

"What does your book say it was?"

"It wasn't scanning the creature. I was trying to work out the origins of this ship."

"And?"

"The Guide says that it originates from a planet a few thousand light years from here," Raph said, looking a bit confused.

"What does it want?" Just asking this made me feel a bit like Raph might know what he was doing. Maybe coming here wasn't an accident, and maybe he knew more than he was telling me.

"She's hiding her real appearance, so I'd guess either she's looked in the mirror or doesn't want to frighten the natives."

"Why *or*? I'd say *and*. Like, she's seen herself in the mirror *and* doesn't want to scare the natives."

I wasn't sure that Raph was listening to me. He was creeping over to the door, or hatch. I pulled up next to him as he said, "I think we need to look into this a bit more. If they are hiding as human...well, you know."

We looked out into a hallway. "It could be bad news for the crew?"

Raph's expression was unreadable. "That's as good a theory as any."

Outside the hatch we crept along a hallway. It was dim, and I thought aloud, "If it's so dark, maybe they see in a different spectrum."

Raph nodded. "Or they don't *see* like we do."

"You mean that the hail could act like a cat's whiskers?"

That impressed Raph. "Good theory, wrong, but good."

Theory number two, but this one is about Raph: he was intentionally keeping stuff back. He knows a lot more about that walking-weather-front than he's telling me. I'm betting that *this* theory's not wrong. "Where are we going?"

"I want to find out why these folks are playing hide-and-go-seek. And I want to start with what kind of weapons they're planning on using."

"Weapons?" I waited for more of an explanation. When I worked out that Raph had finished, I asked, "And?"

"And I think I, or we, actually, will find those answers somewhere towards the front of this ship."

"And how do *you* know this?" I whispered as he led us slowly along.

"A guess."

Our feet were making that sound that you hear when you pull it out of a drying mud puddle. Somewhere something was dripping on a metal surface. The walls were no longer as irregular, but still curved or undulated the length of the corridor. The air smelled of age and anger; it was almost putrid. Soon I found I was timing my steps with the dripping. I was starting to hear my own breathing and heart, like they were screaming in my ear that they still worked.

"Stop." Raph's voice seemed to come from a long way off.

"What is it?" I whispered.

"The air is getting too thin here. We need to go back." Just then we heard something coming down the hall and Raph pulled me around a corner. It sounded like dead twigs dragging across glass. A rasping breath seemed to bear down on us. It was like death was standing just around the corner from us.

A shadow started to grow at our feet. I wanted to see this creeping horror that was scraping towards us, but fear pulled my eyes closed. Just not completely shut. My squinting gaze was almost useless; there wasn't enough light for my eyes to focus. Somewhere there were shapes chafing the ground they passed over and I was blind to them. I listened harder and thought that it sounded like there was something with the creature. We were so exposed there was no way that they could pass without seeing us.

All I wanted to do was run, but where could I go? I was trapped here. I was in a small--tiny--tin spaceship somewhere in the endless, less-than-nothing of space. I was nowhere; I was going to die here. My heart was beating so fast that it felt like it was going to launch right out of my chest. There was one last gasp, and the world went black and silent.

# *LOCK-UP*

I was surprised when I saw Raph standing over me. He was looking down at me and was talking in some language that I didn't understand. I think he was asking me a question, but I had no clear idea of what it was. I did catch the last word, it was "now".

We were no longer in the same hallway, but in a room or chamber. It was metal and was maybe four metres cubed. I was lying on a raised slab in the centre of the room. My mind quickly decided that it was a bed and not something creepier. The walls, floor, and ceiling had a grid of bands and rivets. It was like something you'd see in an old-fashioned ship. Or if I wanted to think darker thoughts, it looked like a cage that someone had sealed up with steel plates. There *was* a door, but I noticed right away there was no handle on this side.

"What happened?" I asked with a weak and shaky voice.

"They found us and captured us," Raph told me.

He sounded as concerned as someone reading the news. There was an emotion in it, but it lacked any sort of genuinity. I'm not sure if that's a real word, but you know what I mean. It was fake. "So that's bad then."

"No, that's good," Raph said with the slightest smirk.

"You sound like you have a plan," I said trying to sit up. I ached all over and had one blinder of a head-ache.

"Don't move for a while. You passed out from hypoxia, oxygen deprivation. You've gotten back to a normal colour, that's a good sign. When they put us in here you looked like the world's tallest smurf." He took my hand and looked at it. "Just stay still, and breathe. The calmer you stay, the quicker you'll feel better."

Raph's eyes didn't have that hunted look in them like I'd have expected. He actually seemed fine, re-laxed and calm. "Do you get locked up a lot?"

"No, actually." He leaned in towards me. "Totally honest, it's been something like centuries. It sort of feels good."

"Great! I'm locked up with *that* sort of guy."

Raph smiled. "Not exactly what I mean. It's just nice not to have read ahead in the Book of Life. I've been doing that for a long while now."

"Centuries? You mean like, *I haven't seen you for a hundred years,* centuries or literally hundreds of years and that is with an '*s*'?"

"The last time I was locked up was, I think, about seven hundred years ago. That's a guess. I mean time in the Library doesn't really move like it does in the universe. I was pretty busy, so I didn't look at my watch a lot."

My headache was starting to fade. "You're not wearing a watch. Don't you have a phone?"

"I did, but I ran out of people to call," he said, and I think he was joking, but there was something sad about him all of a sudden.

"If you're like a gazillion, why do you sound like you're still in school?"

"Good question. I guess because I spend a lot of time talking to myself," Raph told me as he stood up.

"You mean you've been alone for--well, all that time?" I watched his expression change. He now looked at me like a kicked dog. He stopped looking his age and more like an eight-year-old who just dropped his ice cream on the esplanade.

"No, not alone," and then he smiled, and the mood was gone. He suddenly seemed happier than before. "But anyway, I haven't been locked up in a few lifetimes. How you feeling?"

I tried standing up, and I could. "Okay, so how do we get out of this?"

Raph grinned at me. "Ahh...not *yet*. It took a lot to get us locked up. How's about we not ruin it yet."

"You're a cuzband!" I shouted. "A lot of work? And here I was...."

He was back to ignoring me. "What are they doing here?"

I bury my plans to start pounding on him. I mean, he was my way back home. Instead, I said, "Well, they're not daylighting, so that's something."

"Okay...it's been a long time since I've like... talked to someone else...ah...some clarity please?"

"They're hiding, you know, not coming out into the daylight?" I watched Raph start to pace.

"Yeah, I was thinking that, too. They must have come for a reason."

Raph was casting me a line so I bit. "Fine--what reason?"

He stopped walking and shrugged. "No idea, I think we should ask."

"Raph, question for you, but don't freak." I waited for him to say something; he was as blank as the room. So I asked, "Why is it *we* all the time, and not you? Why do *you* think *I* want any part of this *we*?"

"Yeah, good question...okay first of all," he actually started counting on his fingers like a teacher, "you showed up in the Library. There are very few people who can do that, and right now all of them are dead. Second, I wasn't going to leave you alone in the Library. It doesn't know you, and that can be really...well, it's not a great idea. And third, look around, this is cool and wicked fun. Who wouldn't want to do this? I mean just today you've been on two planets and two, count them, two spaceships, and met aliens. Le peche, no?"

"Ah...no, but I get it." It was a straight-up answer, and a lot more than I'd expected. I know we went to school together, but just now when he tried to talk like someone our age, he sounded like an adult doing it. No, it was worse than that; he sounded like an adult trying to sound like a kid. Maybe he really is seven-hundred-plus-years-old. Or--and this is the more likely scenario--maybe he's always been this big a geek. I mean he dresses like he's proud of his school uniform, and he's as tall as a curb. *And* he always has his face in a book. Still he's cooler than I used to think he was. It's like he knows he's awesome but doesn't care.

"Now what?" I asked as I watched him flip a few pages in his book and then tuck it into his belt.

"Now we get some answers," he said and banged on the door a lot harder than I would have expected someone his size, or in fact human, to be able to do.

# THE THRONE ROOM

It was only a matter of a few seconds when three human guards opened the dented hatch. A green gas poured in along the floor. It was only a few centimetres deep, coming up to just above my ankles. I watched it swirl around the room as one of the guards said, "You will come with us."

And we did. The one that spoke led us, the other two following. Raph nodded his head to me as he looked out a long window/portal.

Outside there was another ship off in the distance. There were words writ large on its side. They told me that the ship was the *U.E.C.* गौरव.

"The '*U.E.C.*' part I can read," I whispered to Raph. "So if that's an earth ship, are these folks friendly?"

Raph sort of shrugged. "It's actually a deep-space explorer ship. It may never have been to Earth, but it is a human ship. I'm guessing, or maybe that should be hoping, friendly, but then we may be invisible."

I wasn't ready to think about invisible ships so I asked, "What's *U.E.C.*? Under Earth's Control?"

"It might as well translate to that," Raph sighed and turned his attention to the twisty corridor we were walking along, "It stands for United Earth Consortium."

"Does that mean it's a sort of United Nations spaceship?"

"Yeah, sort of. In the late 21st Century the U.N. sort of changed a bit. It took on some new jobs. Stuff like medical research, space exploration, and you know, stuff like that. It was a big step forward. Although ironically, U.N. also stands for the 'usual nonsense', too."

I don't think that he was taking this situation seriously. "We need a plan."

"We *need* information." His glance over at me suggested that I shut up. I took his hint.

The hall we were walking along could easily do your head in. The floor twisted and turned round-and-round. It basically was a long square-ish, bark-lined, bendy straw, but it turned sideways as well as up and down. I guessed that it did this because gravity was very local.

"How big is this ship?" I asked our group.

None of the soldiers answered, but Raph did. "A bit bigger than two carriers."

And that was bigger than I would have expected. The answer didn't really mean anything to me. I'd only ever seen one aircraft carrier in person. That was on one of those visits to New York. I was about seven. We didn't go aboard; instead we went to a play I think. Anyway, I knew they were big, so this ship was big times two.

It took a while--not that I minded--to get to where we were going. When the corridor ended, we walked into a space that I can only describe as a throne room. The room was long and pod-shaped; its floor sloped upward and the ceiling downward. At the top of the slope, there was a sort of chair hanging over a dais or a platform. The green gas lined the floor here as well. Because of the artificial gravity, it lined the floor without over-filling the lower end where we stood.

There was one of those hail creatures sitting on the throne. Like the other one we saw, its head was a flying mass of snow. The guard in front of us turned and demanded, "Why have you invaded our space?"

I was about to ask what it meant, when Raph said conversationally, "We didn't mean to. Sorry about that."

"We do not believe you," it said. "How did you come here?"

That was the second time someone has asked me that today. I said, "On your matter transmitter."

"It was actually by accident," Raph added.

"You seem to know about us. What are your numbers?"

I worked out that the thing on the throne was talking to us, and that our guard was translating for it. Instead of looking at the guards I started looking at the thing on the throne.

"Just the two of us," Raph told it. "Oh wait, you think we're from the ship out there don't you?" he shook his head. "No. It's like this. We got caught up in a transfer, and then got bounced here. Sorry about that."

Raph suddenly sounded like the guy I'd known in school. Kind of dim, but nice. I think the thing on the throne thought that, too, at least the dim part. The guard said, "Your story will be examined."

Then the two guards from behind circled around and started pushing us out the way we'd come in. Once we were back in the hallway. Raph pulled out a piece of paper. He unfolded it and very casually started fanning the green gas. The front guard stopped and started looking. As soon as he did this Raph stopped.

Back in our cell I started to ask Raph what was going on, but he put his finger to his lips and pointed down to a bit of gas still lingering on the floor. Then he did something more weird than normal. He stood on the bed. He motioned for me to join him. "Raph, why am I standing on a bed?"

"A bed? This isn't a bed, it's a...."

I cut him off. I didn't *want* to know what it was. "It's a bed, okay?" Raph nodded. "Now why am I standing on it?"

"Because I think that gas allows them to monitor us. Did you see what happened when I fanned it?"

"The guards got confused, but why didn't it bother the guy behind? It looked like he could still see you."

"I don't know," Raph admitted without looking too worried about it. "But that's not the important part. I get the feeling that they're in stealth mode. I don't think that human's ship knows it's here."

"But why are they stalking it?"

Raph sounded carefree when he said, "I've no idea."

"I so don't believe that at all. But fine. Now what?" I asked.

"I think we need to get out of here."

That was the best news I'd heard today. "How? And please don't say the air ducts."

Raph hopped down from the bed and walked over to the door. He grabbed one the of the metal bands which ran down the length of the door and with one big pull, the door slid open. He nodded for me to follow. The gas was a lot higher now, about up to my waist. I noticed also the air was much, much thinner. We ran, and I know how ridiculous this sounds, but as he ran Raph was flapping his arms. The gas swirled and eddied. The air was so thin that I was already getting a headache by the time we got to the end of the first hall.

I wanted to ask how far we were going but was afraid to. I didn't know how much they could hear. Also I didn't want to waste my breath. Then I saw the room we'd arrived in. It was like seeing home after a long time away. As we sprinted towards it, the gas became less and less. I literally jumped on the platform while Raph set the controls. Just as we were ready to go, a Hail Creature appeared out of the gas.

Instead of punching the Go button, Raph pulled out his Guidebook and started silently reading at it.

The thing was gliding towards us uber-fast. Its bony arms were stretched out towards us. Its hail seemed to be flying even faster than normal.

"Raph!" I yelled and hit the button for him.

The room around us vanished and we were back in the hangar on the human ship. "Are you insane! You don't read at someone, or some*thing* that's attacking!"

I forgot that we weren't home and dry. We were now intruders on another ship. I didn't bother to count the number of guns that were pointing at us.

# MISSED, BIG TIME

We weren't exactly locked up again. I mean the door was closed, but I got the impression it was unlocked. The armed guards just outside it made the lock unnecessary. Instead of a king or queen sitting on a throne there was a colonel standing over us. "I said who are you?"

Raph smiled. I got the impression that he had done this sort of thing more than he was willing to admit. "I told you. I'm Raph and this is Lang."

"That's not the right answer." The colonel was not yelling, but I got the impression he might start soon.

I could tell that Raph was just winding the guy up tighter and tighter. "I think the problem is that you're not asking the right question."

I could see the tension building around the colonel's eyes. He was starting to squint. "Where are you from?"

I wanted to say that I was from Earth, but I didn't know what year it was here. I had a feeling it wasn't the 21st Century. So I stayed quiet as Raph kept up whatever he was doing. "That's a far better one. The Library."

The colonel took a deep breath. "What is that supposed to mean?"

"It's a place where one stores information," Raph said with a smile.

"So you're spies?"

Raph's smile got a little broader. "If you'd like; I tend to think of us as researchers."

"We shoot spies," the colonel told us with a bit of a sneer.

"Oh well, that's just great," I said to Raph. "This is all your fault. I should be home by now. Thanks."

"So you've been kidnapped?" the man asked.

"No," I said and then realized that Raph wasn't just winding *him* up; he was doing it to me too. "I was at home and then I was with him in the Library, and then we were on Mars, and then we were here."

"Mars?" The man looked worried for only a fraction of a second, but it was without a doubt a worried look. So Mars was important in all this. I suddenly had a lot more respect for Raph.

"We're researchers," Raph said calmly. "Mars is a very interesting place."

I think that comment put us above the guy's pay-grade, because he turned and walked out of our holding room. The room looked like you'd expect a room on a military ship to look. It was drab with a table and four chairs. I didn't see any cameras, but I assumed they were there. I guess camera is probably a dated term by now.

"So what type of surveillance system do they have in here?" I asked Raph, who was leaning back on his chair looking up at the ceiling.

"Walls, floors, and ceiling act as scanners and are creating a full, 3D model of this room a few metres away from here. Currently four people are watching us. One is recording the interview and doing facial scans to verify our identities; one is checking and cross-referencing every word we say. Two people are walking around this projection wondering who we are, and the one with their hands behind their back is the more worried of the two."

I couldn't tell if he was making it up or just showing off again. "What's *their* next move?"

Raph looked at me and grinned. "No idea."

"I guess we wait then." Everything about his expression said the opposite. I leaned back in my chair too, and started whistling.

We did wait, but for less time than it felt. When you've nothing on your mind but the passing of time, time passes slowly. When the door opened it wasn't the colonel from before, but it was a woman in a business suit. Nice to see that some things haven't changed. It was not exactly like what I imagined a business person from the future would wear, but it was close enough.

She sat down as Raph returned his chair to all four legs. The room was silent as she watched Raph smile at her. There was the slightest change in her expression just before Raph said, "I'm not on record."

"What do you mean?" she asked.

"I mean that you scanned us and looked for us on the personnel records, and when that came up blank you came in here to look for surgical alterations that would appear at the sub-dermal level. But you just found nothing. Also you've confirmed that my friend here is using a what," Raph looked up at the ceiling and counted, "about a two hundred and fifty year-old identity. You figure that it is our first mistake, but can't figure out what it might mean."

"You seem to know a lot about us," the woman said.

Raph smiled back at her, and I said, "He likes showing off."

"He does it well," she said looking at me for the first time.

"I don't have any sub-dermal-level scarring either. What I do have is a name. I'm Lang."

"Of course you are," the woman said with an expression that showed she was willing to play along. "My name is Bellentha."

"Is that a first name or a surname?" I asked.

Raph leaned over to me and whispered loud enough for everyone to hear, "Her first name is General."

"Umm," I stammered.

Raph cut in, "So we're not on the *Pride*. Which ship is this?"

The General looked concerned. "We're on the *U.E.C. Adventure*. Why would you say the *Pride*? The

*Pride* was lost six months ago. As you well know, I'm sure."

"Only it wasn't," Raph assured her.

I leaned over to him this time. "Is that the ship--"

Before I could finish, Raph said, "It is."

Bellentha smiled like we'd just given something away. "So you saw the *Pride*."

Raph leaned forward. "We did, and I think you have a problem."

"And what problem is that?"

"No," Raph said and leaned back.

"Okay." The General stood up. "Kill them."

"What!" I shouted. "I've got things I still need to do. Dying isn't one of them."

Bellentha looked over at me. "Him first." The guard pulled out his weapon and aimed it at my head. "Raph do something."

"I don't have to. There is a protocol on this ship that stops energy weapons from firing. A disable order has to be issued from the command deck."

The General looked impressed. "I turned it off before I came down. Guard, on the count of three."

Raph looked bored as she started counting. The guy was mental. "Three. Two."

"Raph!" I begged.

"One!"

I nearly peed myself I was so scared, but nothing happened. Finally Raph said, "You could have turned it off, but it would re-activate after five minutes. You've been here for almost six. And before you embarrass everyone by saying that you could have issued a 'general battle stations' command," Raph continued and pointed at the gun. "The indicator light on the guard's firearm is not illuminated. So no general command is standing."

"So you are part of Earth Intelligence," the General said to Raph. "Guard, stow your fire arm."

"We saw the *Pride*," Raph said, "And we saw what was travelling with her."

This time the General didn't bother bluffing. "She is travelling alone."

"No. There's another ship with her," I said before Raph had the chance.

"I don't know who you are, or what your part in this is, but no ship would chance that."

"And yet we saw another ship."

"Why? What's on-board that is so bad?" I asked.

The General continued to look at Raph. "He is obviously not part of E. I. so I won't be talking about it in front of him."

She was right about me and wrong about Raph. I got the feeling that this was another one of his acts. It made me doubt everything he'd said. I had to trust him because he was my only way back home, but I didn't have to like it.

"My friend and I need our things back, and a place to rest for a few hours," Raph said rising to his feet. He was quite a lot shorter than the General but still seemed to loom over her.

Wordlessly the General turned and walked out of the room. As she left, a guard came in and handed Raph his Guidebook and me my keys and wallet. "This way please."

The hallways on this ship were normal, and long. I was getting a bit bored as we walked, and my mind started to wander. I kept smelling something sweet, almost rotten. I noticed it every time we passed a crossing hallway. Finally we reached the end of the corridor. I'd had just realized that there were no doors in this area when the guard turned on us. The odor was coming from him. Now that he had stopped there was a slight bit of green gas collecting at his feet.

He moved fast, but Raph moved faster. He pushed me aside. The man's weapon actually looked like an electric razor, but I figured he was not going to shave me. Instead, three beams of blue light shot out. They hit the wall just past my shoulder, melting the metal away.

"Oh damn!" I yelled as Raph grabbed the man's arm and did something to it. A second later the guard was dead and his arm was part of the wall next to us. I'd never seen a dead body before. I just stood there staring at it.

"Come on," Raph said and pulled me along behind him. I looked once the way we came; the guard was gone. Turning back to Raph to tell him this important piece of information I ploughed into him. He had suddenly come to a stop and I almost knocked him off his feet. He opened a sliding door and pushed me in. Before I could say anything he clamped his hand over my mouth. Then with is free hand he opened his Guidebook and flipped a few pages. I guess he found what he was looking for because he took his hand away from my mouth. He ran a finger down the page and then breathed a sigh of relief. "Okay we can stay here for a little while."

"What the hell was that all about?"

Raph smiled. "Finding answers."

# QUESTIONING RAPH

Like everyone else on this ship I was ready to kill Raph. "What the hell have you dragged me into?"

"My first guess would be an invasion, but there are a few things that don't add up."

"Okay what are you, Sherlock?" I asked looking around.

"Like I said to the General, I'm a researcher." he added, "and a sort of time grafter. But that's the part people don't need to know about."

I was sure this was another act. "A what?"

"Someone who steps in when time-events go off the rails."

We were in a storage closet of some sort. "Has time gone off the rails here?"

"Think so," he said opening his Guide and reading aloud. "Okay, the creatures we met are called the Hagl. Hmmm, they come from a planet nowhere near here."

"Yeah, some thousands of light years away, right?" I whispered.

"Yes, and...okay. They seem to be explorers or conquerors. It's hard to translate that word, maybe imperialist would work."

"Raph, do you know what's going on here?" I asked. I was feeling like my understanding of everything that had happened since I walked into the Library was a blur. It was all connected in some way, but I was blank on how.

He looked up at me with a surprisedly shocked look. "Of course not."

"But all that stuff with the General?"

"I know a lot of trivia. And there's *always* someone walking around with their hands behind their backs. The nice thing about hierarchies is that information is compartmentalized. It's all boxed up and locked away. If you seem to have a key, then people believe you're one of them. The obvious facts are often over looked.

"The real story has to do with this ship and the *Pride*--that other Human ship we saw--and what they have to do with Mars. But right now the most important piece to this puzzle is, what's your part in all this?"

"Me?" It really was the last thing I'd expected to be asked.

"Yes you. I was ready for retirement, and then you show up. There is something about you that the Library thinks is important."

I took a step back. "Ask the Library. How should I know?"

He said looking pretty angry. "I'm asking you."

I may be out in the middle of space, two hundred years from home, but I was *not* going to be bullied by a guy with a travel guide. Particularly one that four months ago couldn't find Madagascar on a map! "I don't know! You're the 'expert'! You figure it."

And then all of that bravado was gone. "Okay, we'll let that one go for a bit. Let's get some answers about the *Pride*."

Unsure of what to say, I asked, "So how?"

"We've a few options." He started on the fingers again. "First, jump back to the Hagl and ask them. Second, we find a Hagl here and ask him or her. Third, we ask the General, assuming that she's not a

Hagl. If she is, then we're back to number two. Or four, or three depending on your ideas about the General, we ask the ship's information system. Oh, and then there's five, run until we get some answers."

"Does five work?" I asked, not sure if he was joking or not.

Raph smiled. "Surprisingly well."

Just then we heard people coming along the hallway outside. I stared at the door and said, "Something tells me it's going to be five."

"It normally is," Raph admitted as he slid the door open a crack to see what was going on. "Okay, time to go!"

We ran out into the hallway, and then started a random left-right pattern that led us back towards the hangar. My heart was beating so fast that I was surprised that it was staying in place. It had a lot less to do with the running and a lot more about the panic I was feeling.

We didn't see another living soul all the way there. It was like we were running in a ghost ship. It seemed impossible, but then I remembered that this was a spaceship. Maybe in space they don't have to stack people like cord-wood. Maybe, or maybe something else was happening. As we ran, I got the impression that Raph knew exactly how to get from here to there. At first it seemed like we were just running away, but now it was clear that we had also been running *to* somewhere.

When we got to the hangar we ducked behind a stack of crates. There *were* people here, just like before. "Okay so, you've a plan. What is it?"

"We need to get to the *U.E.C. Pride*," he said pulling out his Guide and scanning with it.

"I thought we needed to get back to Mars, so I can get home."

Raph looked at me and shook his head. "The universe is out here. The whole thing. Don't you want to see more of it?"

"Okay, the parts I've seen seem to be filled with people just a bit too willing to shoot me."

"Hand on my heart, that's the way it works sometimes. But hey that's adventure. Do you really want to just go lay under a tree somewhere? This type of stuff gets your heart pumping, right?"

"This sort of stuff seems to be a really good way to make sure that my heart *stops* pumping."

"Chill, we made it here. We'll make it the rest of the way," Raph said actually sounding like someone our age for the first time.

"Have you always done this stuff on your own?" I asked as he started flipping pages.

"No. I used to do it with friends."

"What happened to them?" I asked.

"They died."

"They died!?" I choked out, and then hissed, "And then you wonder why I'm not into this?"

Raph looked at me like he was having a problem understanding what I was talking about. "It was a long time ago."

"Are they still dead?" I asked, my voice almost cracking with frustration.

Raph nodded. "Yeah."

"Then I don't care! Dead is dead!"

His face dropped from being overly cheerful to one filled with painful memories. "Okay, I used to hang with a group called the Elementals. They saved the universe, *a lot*. Eventually after a few hundred years they died off, and I was left on my own. That was seven hundred years or a few days ago. It depends which way round you go," Raph said still flipping through his book.

"Raph!" I didn't exactly yell, but sort of snapped. I couldn't believe we were doing this here in a hangar. "I need to know right now! Do you have a plan!"

"Yes," he snapped back.

"Good. What is it, and when does it involve me getting back home?"

"Ah...it's in progress, and I don't think I can," he said looking up at me.

"Okay, in your weird and freaky world does 'yes' actually mean 'no'? And what do you mean 'you can't'?" I said but he was already shaking his head. "Stop that."

"Van, I'm sorry. I won't be able to get you home. At least not back to where we grew up."

He called me Van. That is what my friends *actually* call me. I think it means he does remember me. "Why? Why can't I go home?"

"It's like this, there are points in time that are really weak, or thin. Every time the Library opens a Portal it moves things around. If that happens at one of these thin points there might be a rupture and the whole of everything would get sucked away. I'm sorry we can't chance it. The Library pulled you out of your chronostream for a reason. I don't know what it is, but I do know that it means something." He was being dead straight.

He looked really, truly, sorry. I didn't know what a chronostream was. Chrono means time and space

event, like he said. Stream, well that's obvious. So...oh I get it, my timeline, the days I'd live if one day followed another and not like this. I changed the subject. "What about the plan?"

"Like I said, everything seems to revolve around the *Pride*. We need to get there. Over there is the pad we need to use."

"Really? Over there? Over there where the guards are standing? That *over there*?"

"That'd be the one," he said with a nod.

"And if they see us...?"

"They'll shoot to kill," he said in the way other people say *good morning*. Panic started to bubble up inside me. "Just make sure they don't."

We ran in that way you see in movies. The sort of way that when you see it, you think: there is no way someone is *not* going to see that. I was shocked out of my pants that we made it.

Raph did something weird then. He pulled out a bookmark from this Guide and laid it on the key pad. A second later the MaTeS lighted up.

"Ready?" he whispered.

"Yes!" Someone must have seen the lights from the MaTeS because that's when people started coming at us. We dived onto the platform and a second later everyone had vanished.

# SOIL AND SOLDIERS

Okay they didn't disappear, we had, but that wasn't obvious from my perspective. We had made it to the *Pride*, but the two ships looked so alike that I hadn't noticed the slight and subtle differences for a few seconds.

The MaTeS trip made me feel sick to my stomach. As I went to get up, I accidently leapt up off the platform by about a metre and a half. I freaked, as I slowly landed. "What? I can fly?"

Raph got up slowly. "We're in a Welcome Ship. They keep the gravity pretty low in the storage blocks. It might make you feel a bit sick in your tum."

"Okay, nobody over the age of seven, or below the age of thirty uses the word 'tum'," I insisted. "Is this the *Pride*?" I asked checking how much gravity there was by doing slight hops.

The expression that Raph gave me was something like you'd expect to see from a cool kid in school--when you're a puddle of green slime. He pointed to the four-metre-tall letters reading, 'गौरव' scrolled along the wall. "Duh."

"Okay," I said, defending green slime everywhere. "I don't read...whatever language that is."

Raph looked sincerely surprised. "Really? Didn't I add you to the Translator setting?"

He started messing around with his Guide again. He was right at the back of it, like he was looking up something in the index. He started poking at the book. "Okay, can you read it now?"

I looked over at the wall, but it still looked the same. There was a change though. Suddenly I knew that the MaTeS that I was still standing on was actually called a Matter Transference System. That it was invented fifty years ago by a woman named Serene Flaenaf. That her theory was based on papers written...

I stopped. Information was coming in so quickly that it was like scrolling down pages and pages of text. There was no way I could remember it all.

Raph looked up from his book. "How's that?"

"No change, but I know things that I shouldn't. I mean like that the Guide's Translator helps you and me understand Alien and stuff."

He tapped a few more time before he said, "Hell, I'll just give you the full profile. Don't think anything too stupid, like what's going to happen next. That's like Rule One of Time Grafting. If you try to predict the future bad things will happen."

"It's not working."

"Really?" he said looking back at his Guide. "How can you tell?"

"'Cause' I'm still hearing you talking in non-sense."

"Yeah, well," he closed the book and looked around, "There is only so much that the Translator can do. You'll have to make a bit of effort."

I caught his smirk, and it was all le peche between us. Whatever he did seemed to finally work. I could read the name of the ship now. "But wait, what were the aliens talking in? I mean, how did I understand them?"

"I'd set the Translator to default earlier," Raph said, stuffing his Guide into his belt and covering it with his shirt.

"Default. Got it," I said looking around the cargo hold. "So now what?"

"We explore." Raph stepped down from the MaTeS' platform and started walking; I followed.

I thought: We should go look around for someone. There is no reason to hang around an empty room. I want to find someone and tell them why we are here. It is about time that we 'fessed up to all this. I just want to find them. I want to *make* them listen to us.

That thought stopped me in my tracks. I wanted to *make* them? That didn't sound like me.

Raph stopped walking, too. "There's something here."

"All I see is a big empty room. We need to stop wasting time and find someone," I said, and I actually sounded, what? Scared, or maybe angry?

"You want to get out of here?" His voice was infuriatingly calm.

"I just said that, didn't I?" Wow, this guy can be so thick!

"Why?" he asked in a way that made me want to punch him in the face.

"How dumb is that question?"

"Why do you want to find someone? I mean the last two times we've found someone, they've wanted to kill us. Doesn't make much sense to me," he said.

"That's because...." I was going to say something really rude, but why? He was right. We've been running away from people lately, why was I so eager all of sudden to try to find someone? "I...I don't know."

"Like I said, I think there is something here. My guess is that it's some sort of Avoidance Field." Raph must have seen my confused expression because he explained. "It's a field that activates the natural flee instinct in all of us. It stops us from thinking clearly."

I shifted my eyes around like I knew a predator was stalking me. "So is that what's here?"

Raph nodded. He was also standing dead still, but he was turning his head. Like he was listening for something. "I think the field is here to put people off nosing about."

"Couldn't your Guide just tell you what's here?" I asked, still not totally sure that staying here was a good idea.

"Maybe," he admitted, "but where's the fun in that? Do you know how long it's been since--? Have I said that before?" I nodded this time, and Raph shrugged. "That's life. So let's get on with this."

We sort of wandered around the hangar in a random pattern until the feeling that we should run got stronger, and that's the direction where we would head. Finally, about halfway across the bay Raph stopped and started groping around. His eyes were open, but he was acting like he'd just gone blind.

With a slight thump he stopped. It sounded like he touched something but there was nothing there. He looked like a mime who'd found an imaginary wall to play with. Then suddenly his hand shot forward and he ripped something away. There was the sound of fabric pulling away, and all of a sudden there were crates in front of us.

"What the heck?" I said with a jump back. The Avoidance Field was still affecting me.

I could feel the Translator working. I knew that these large plastic pyramid-shaped crates were filled with !$*%, but that didn't mean anything to me. I tried getting more information but there was nothing else coming.

It was weird to have something working or thinking in my head. It was like thoughts were coming to me that obviously weren't mine, but made sense to me. Or, they made sense of the world for me.

Maybe this is what it's like to be mental. It's not *that* bad actually.

"Okay, I can read the labels, but I still don't know what it means."

Raph ran his hand over a stack of the pyramids. "They're full of drilling soil."

I was getting used to the idea of not only not knowing what things were, but also not understanding the explanation. It was like reading a dictionary and having to look up the words in the definition. "Okay, and what's that when it's got it's pants on?"

Raph disappeared behind another stack. "It's a type of soil-based acid. It's a lightweight way of digging very deep holes."

"But why hide it? Is it a weapon?" I asked.

"Good questions. Maybe it has something to do with the fact this is a military ship."

He was getting at something that I was missing. "So?"

"The last two ships we've been on have been teaming, I mean like bursting, with people."

Now I understood. "And if this is another military ship, where is everyone?"

"Don't you think we've been out in the open for enough time for someone to notice us,?"

"Could the ship be on automatic?"

Raph shrugged. "Maybe. You think we should find out?"

"It's seems like the next thing to do, so yeah," I said, and we walked out across the cargo hold to find someone in charge.

"I think we should head towards the middle of the ship. The Bridge should be there," Raph said as we started to weave along the grid of hallways

"I thought it would be at the top of the ship."

Raph stopped and smiled, shaking his head. "You know you sound just like I used to," he started walking at a pace that was something between a stroll and quickstep. "On earth in the days when ships sailed the seas and needed to look out ahead of them bridges were at the highest point because they needed to see as far ahead as they could. Also the water could be dangerous. But now...."

"They are in the middle of the ship because-- space isn't something you want to be right up next to," I finished.

"Got it in one," Raph complimented.

Despite the similarities of their holds, the *Pride* and the *Adventure* were very different. The halls were not metal but plastic. There were bright colours everywhere. The lights were so bright that if I closed my eyes it felt like I was outside. I'd bet in deep space that would be a feeling people would miss.

With that in mind I started looking around for other design details. I started to notice that each hallway was different. Some had curved ceilings, while others soft floors. In fact none of the hallways were exactly the same. There was a huge variety. There were lots of things I was missing. I got the impression that it would take a lot of time and effort to see everything just in this one corridor. Maybe that was what the designers and builders were aiming for. Who knows how long the crew would be aboard. People would go crazy if everything looked the same.

As we walked, something I'd thought about earlier came back to me. "Raph? When we ran from our hiding place to the MaTeS did you know where we were going?"

"Yeah. I mapped out the ship after we got captured," he said looking around as we walked.

"How? The first thing they did was to take your Guide?"

Raph smiled. "There are ways to have limited communication with a Guide without actually holding it in your hands."

That made sense to me. It was a pretty advanced bit of tech. "Okay. Did you plot a course that somehow avoided everyone else?"

"No," Raph said with the shake of his head.

"Then where did everyone go when we were running?" I asked feeling more than a little worried about how people kept disappearing and reappearing.

"No idea." He glanced over at me, but didn't continue. A second later we heard the sound of people running. "Okay let me take the lead on this," Raph said.

I laughed to myself. *As if it's ever gone the other way,* I thought, but said, "You bet, Big Coona."

That derailed Raph. He suddenly looked a lot less focused. He stopped and looked up at the ceiling, "Coona? No, I think that's Kahuna."

"So what's a Kahuna then?" I asked as two uniformed soldiers or security guards came around the corner. They looked like soldiers, but they also looked like they had only just gotten their boots on. I guess they weren't expecting two guys to just pop in, literally.

Raph ignored them. "No idea. Just an expression I guess. It sounds like it might be Hawaiian."

"Freeze!" the guard on the left shouted.

Raph rolled his eyes. "What do you think we were doing?"

"It seems too warm to freeze here," I said to Raph.

"Good point. By the way, in the realm of bad semantics, did you know there's a game called Two-Person Solitaire? I never really got that."

"Where did you come from!" The guard on the right shouted. Her voice almost screeching.

"Back there," Raph pointed behind us. "We were making our way to the Bridge. Do you know the way?"

Both soldiers looked confused. The one on the left raised the visor on his helmet. He clearly had gotten over the shock of our appearance. "What are you doing here?"

Raph smiled. "Thanks for asking. You know a lot of times people don't start out nice. So, do you know there's a massive spaceship off your starboard side, or do you say right-side these days?"

"We say even-quadrant. The ship you saw is our escort. Where did you say you're from?"

"We're from Biblia, and that's not the ship we were talking about."

Biblia? Where the heck was that? It sounded a bit like...oh I get it. We're from the Library, but that doesn't sound like a planet. And then I thought of something else. "Like odd on the left and even on the right. Do you also have front and back co-ordinance?"

The soldier on the right now said, "If there were eight of them, they wouldn't be quadrants would they?"

"Good point," I admitted.

"The ship that I'm talking about isn't from around here. And the people on board...I think *you'd* call them creatures."

"How did you find it?" the second one asked. He was about the same size as his partner.

Before Raph could answer that, the first guard said, "We haven't picked up anything."

"Are you looking?" There was that type of silence that can only be called embarrassed silence. "We can give you a rough area where to look if you'd like."

The two soldiers looked at one another as if to say, *I guess it would be okay.* The male guard spoke for both of them. "Show me."

As we all walked to wherever we were going, conversation started. Both of them seemed nice enough. The soldier who had been on the right took off her helmet; out fell long waves of blonde hair. She was taller than me by about the same height that I was taller than Raph. I got the impression that these two were more scientists than guards. Both of them were wearing perfume, and neither gave off that twitchy, move-and-I'll-shoot vibe. Oh man, was I wrong.

# THE TROUBLE WITH NEW FRIENDS

When Raph, our two soldier friends, and I entered the ship's bridge I admit that I was expecting something from Star Trek. All bright and shiny, a Hollywood glossy version of a water ship's deck. Instead it was more like I was on the inside of a ball. There were walking paths between desk stations all the way around the sphere. There were other doors around the "room" One of them was directly at the top of the place.

We walked into the room on a ramp that twisted us around on to the room's floor; it was part wheelchair ramp and part rollercoaster track. Its effect on my stomach was a lot more like the rollercoaster part. As I twisted, or gravity twisted, my stomach had to try to keep up. I thought how funny it would be if every time someone walked onto the bridge in a movie, they threw-up.

The more senior of the soldiers led Raph to a workstation not too far around the room. I turned to the one next to me.

"Is it just the two of you around here?" I asked.

She smiled. "Yes. Just the two of us here, but there are others aboard. Don't think of trying anything."

"Never even thought of thinking of it. I'm Lang." I think I surprised her because she was conversation walling with a blank stare. "This is the point where you tell me your name."

"Oh, yes. I see. I am Re-beca," she said, just that way. Like it was something she had to think about.

"Do friends call you Re-beca, or Beca?"

"My--social peers are friends? Yes, they call me that."

Okay, humans have changed a bit since, well however long it's been from my time to now. Yeah...*humans* have changed. "Raph, I think I need to call in that everything is okay here." I yelled up to him, adding, "not?"

Raph turned to me, "Yeah, good idea. Right behind you."

I turned and punched the soldier next to me. At least I tried but my fist passed right through her head. But it affected the Hagl's camouflage enough to let me see that she was definitely not human. At the same time I did that, Raph literally launched himself towards me. Because of the weird gravity he ended up landing right at the door.

"Time to go!" he shouted and ran out the door.

I was right on his heels. "Are they both Hagl?"

We rounded a corner a lot faster than we should have and did the hallway-slam again. We collapsed into a pile of arms and legs. As we extracted ourselves from one another, Raph said, "I think they might have just replaced the guards before we got here."

"Thanks Captain Obvious, and here I was thinking that is was because they'd met you before!" We started running again.

"Yeah okay it could be that, too. At least we know why they looked like--." And just then is when we saw another guard running towards us from the opposite direction. "Stop them!" someone yelled from behind us. No award for guessing who shouted that.

I jumped at the soldier in front of us and punched her, while Raph grabbed her weapon. My hand collided with flesh and bone, meaning that this was a real human. At the same time Raph rolled and shot at the two soldiers chasing us. He was a *good* shot.

The first blast hit the leading human-looking Hagl in the chest and threw her backward into the other. His second blast made sure that neither of them was going to get up again.

"Nice to run into you," Raph said pulling the guard to her feet.

She was fast to assess the situation. She saw us and she saw the now-transformed Hagl; they were rotting away. "What are those things, and who the heck are you?"

"Their Hagl," I said as Raph ignored this new soldier and her questions. He walked over to the fading creatures.

She looked at me like...well, like I was someone who had just punched her in the face, taken her weapon, then and shot two aliens that I'm betting looked like people she knew. So she had a bit of a grumpy face. "Start talking or I swear you'll be in for a world of pain."

"I'm Lang, and that's Raph," I told her. "We discovered a Hagl ship shadowing you, and we came to warn you. But we met them. They were already here. So we ran, met you, and handled it. Sorry about hittin' you. I wasn't sure that you weren't one of them. They have these sort of...." I stopped talking because she'd obviously stopped listening.

"Believe me. We'll talk about that later," she assured me. She was my height and with her armour on was a bit wider than me. I wasn't looking forward to that conversation. I had the feeling I would walk away from it the less well-off.

I tried to get her mind off me punching her. "Is there anyone else on the ship?"

"We're on remote control. There were only three of us aboard, but I'm guessing that you knew that."

"Yeah, *I* did," Raph said. He was crouching over what was left of the Hagls. His Guide was out and he was flipping pages fast. I didn't know what he was scanning for. His Guide *did* tell me that he was recording data which could be used later.

"*You* might have known, but I didn't. Like I didn't know she was human."

"Knew that, too," Raph called back.

"*You* might have, but *I'm* the one apologizing, and *I* didn't," I said to Raph, shaking my head as I said to the new, *human* soldier, "Sorry about punching you, by the way, did I say that I'm Lang."

"Tulla," she said, proving that humans haven't changed *that* much since my time.

We stood there in silence again for about a minute before I repeated, "I'm really sorry."

"What are you two?" Tulla asked instead of accepting my apology.

"Human," I said, trying to sound casual.

She ignored that answer. "Are you Specials, or Private, or what?"

"Oh," I said, now understanding the question.

Before I could tell her that she had it all wrong, Raph stood up. The Hagl were gone; only two damp and stained uniforms remained. "We're Specials. I think we need more information about this ship. You're the last one alive on this one, did you know that the remote signal you're following is not from the *Adventure* but from the Hagl's ship?"

Tulla was about to answer when her brain caught up with her mouth and she closed it. After obvious reconsideration she asked, "How do you know?"

"We've been on the Bridge. I think the Hagl wanted to see how I detected them before they killed us," Raph said as he stuffed his hands in his pockets.

"Other than the drilling soil, what's on board?" I asked Tulla.

"Drilling soil? We don't have that on board," she insisted.

Five minutes later the three of us were standing in front of the pyramid containers. "I don't understand. Why are they here? They can't be."

"Well, we didn't bring them," I said.

Raph added, "Plus the Avoidance Field would have to be wired into the main power grid, someone would have noticed. I think they have been here for a long time."

"Didn't the General say that this ship had been lost?" I asked Raph, but Tulla answered.

"It was on a deep-space tour," Tulla started but Raph finished for her.

"And it stopped sending its PiOnS, or Point Operational Signal. You assumed the worse, and then a few weeks ago it showed up on edge scans. The *Adventure* was sent out to tow it back." I could actually feel Raph pulling the data in from his Guide. He must have scanned the *Adventure*'s network for standing orders.

"Okay so you know our mission, but...." Tulla didn't need to actually ask her question.

"What are we doing here?" Raph asked with a smile on his face. "We're here to make sure your mission fails."

# TRUTH AND LIES

Tulla pulled her gun so fast that there was no way either Raph or I could have defended ourselves. "You're going to do what?"

I was thinking the same thing as Raph said, "Your ship is not being guided by the *Adventure*. It's being led, by the nose, by the Hagl ship."

"Why would you even try lying like that? It can't be," Tulla insisted but Raph has this way of knowing exactly how to get into people's heads.

"Why do you think the Hagl were here?" he said like a teacher talking to a student who was not meeting his expectations. "They were trying to stop us? I was able to pinpoint the direction the tractor beam was coming from, despite their best efforts."

It took Tulla a second to look for a gap in Raph's story. I'm guessing she couldn't find one because she said, "But why?"

"Maybe there is something else on board. Something that the Hagl want to have, or...." I thought out loud.

"Or they're delivering something that Earth might not like," Raph finished.

Tulla got this sly look. "I don't think so."

"Why don't you contact the General? She'd know," Raph offered.

His suggestion seemed innocent enough to me, but Tulla glared at him. "You know I can't do that."

Raph grinned. "Really?"

"There is a communication ban active until we get past M...our marker."

"You've a bit of a stutter there?" Raph noted.

Tulla watched Raph carefully. "You know about the gag don't you."

"Until you get to Mars? Yes." He was such a cheater. The Guide was feeding him information almost constantly. On the other hand, I had to give him full-likes for his ability to pull out the relevant search terms from Tulla.

"So why ask for me to call the General?" I think she was starting to believe us.

"Because if you'd try, you'd find that you couldn't reach them. The Hagl are blocking your communication bandwidth," Raph said losing his smile.

"And no one would notice because there isn't supposed to be any communication." I was starting to get the hang of this plan.

Tulla looked around the hangar. "This is just an old deep-space ship."

"And the cover story is?" I asked.

"The ship needs to be analyzed for leads that might explain how it ended up heading home without a crew," Raph told me.

"It's not a cover story," Tulla insisted.

"Isn't it? Really? Why wasn't it examined at Luyten? It has everything needed for something like this," Raph offered.

Tulla was starting to look shaken. "Why do you think?"

"Because, like I said, there is something else here." I could tell that Raph had just about convinced her.

"But what you're suggesting can't happen," Tulla was almost pleading. "People would know if something was being smuggled through Earth's defences."

"Well," I pointed at the containers of soil, "these were here, and I'm guessing that only the wrong people knew about them."

That seemed to clinch it for her. Tulla's whole demeanour changed. She was again a soldier with a mission. "I'll sweep quadrant one, you two keep to here in quadrant four. We'll meet up again after we've finished them." I was tempted to salute. "Do you both have your coms?"

The word 'com' was quickly translated for me to the word 'phone'. "Ah, no. I sort of was called in at the last minute."

Tulla pulled out something that looked very much like my phone and handed it to me. "I'll get an extra from the Bridge."

Raph and I watched her walk away. "Is she really going to the Bridge to get a com?"

"What do you think?" Raph asked.

"I think she's going to break radio silence. How did you know that it was blocked? I didn't feel that information come in."

"Because I set it that way," Raph admitted. "I re-focused the transmitter to receive the tractor beam signal."

We started walking in the opposite direction from Tulla. "That was clever."

Raph shrugged, "Lucky really. I was hoping that the *Adventure* would be able to pick up the change, but I have a feeling the Hagl are well-placed over there."

"You mean you think the General is a Hagl?" I was more than a bit surprised by that.

"Maybe, or someone very close to her. Either way, the *Adventure* has no idea it's heading into a trap."

# UNWELCOME CARGO

The cargo area was huge and took up most of the cube part of the ship. But the ring that made up the rest of it was even bigger. Passing from one to the other was like waiting for a lift. There were sliding doors that counted down. When the number reached zero the doors opened and then a few seconds later slid shut. Instead of feeling like we were going up or down it felt like we turned and got heavier. Then the doors slid open again. On the other side was a bright hallway. I felt heavy-footed, like when you step off a trampoline and try to jump. Gravity was obviously back to normal, if not a bit more.

I walked down the corridor looking in door after door. "What are you doing?" Raph asked, not looking around but at his Guide.

"I'm looking for something out of place. What are you doing?"

Raph looked up and turned slightly. "What do you think I'm doing?"

I thought about it and then understood what his Guide was telling me. "Oh, you're scanning for objects that don't belong on an Earth ship. You know I don't know if I like having your Guide in my head."

"It'll feel less weird when you have your own."

I wasn't sure what to say about that. The idea that he was so certain that I'd start doing this as a full-timer was a bit more than I was willing to take. Anyway that made me think of a question I'd had for a long time. "Why *are* we helping? I mean, things happen all the time. You're not always there making sure no one gets hurt, or in fact shooting up the aliens."

Raph looked at me like an old man about to justify his life. "Why are we here? I'm not sure. I, or we, get pulled in when something is happening in time that shouldn't."

"Is something going wrong here? And anyway I thought that if something changes that it's all okay. I mean, isn't there supposed to be an infinite number of universes where every possibility can or has happened?"

With a sigh Raph said, "Yes, I think there is something wrong with time. The rest of it is all just nonsense. In your time, the "high priests" of mathematics thought theirs was the only tool in the universe. It's not, it's only one of...." A sort of psychic ping from the Guide stopped Raph in mid-flow. "I think I might have found something."

"Should I call Tulla?" I asked pulling out the com she gave me.

Raph shook his head. "She's probably still on the Bridge trying to call the *Adventure*. Let's give her a chance to get to her quadrant, make up a cover story, and call us."

I eyed him carefully. "You know, sometimes I think *you* think I'm an idiot. That wouldn't make any sense. First off, if you were telling her the truth, she won't be able to contact the *Adventure*. If we wait she'll be further away, and what do you mean cover story?"

Raph asked, raising one eyebrow, "Where would you go if two people showed up out of nowhere, shot two comrades, and then told you that you'd been lied to?"

I nodded. "Yeah, I'd go the Bridge and try to report in. But the ship-to-ship coms are down you said."

"They are, but the *Adventure* is almost in shouting distance. A personal com could reach if you were on the correct side of the ship, like quadrant one is. And what do you think they'll tell her?"

Raph kept looking at me like he was expecting a straightforward and clear answer. "We're lying."

"Right, she'll call us to find out where we are, and then start hunting us. So would you prefer to start the race of finding the alien device before she finds us, or start the clock now and make it fairer for her?"

I like people being honest with me, and I like letting them know where I stand with them. I was the guy in school that always tried to look at both sides of the argument, but there are limits. "I don't know if I like the idea of people hunting me. Straight up, I'd prefer the lead. I'll deal with the rest after that."

Raph smiled, "Good answer. In our business, forthrightness is about the best we can hope for."
We followed the Guide's direction around the ship. Behind a door marked "Caution! High-Risk Radiation!" was something very alien. It was a ball-shaped

pod, maybe. It looked like a cross between a seed and a bucky-ball. And it was glowing.

Raph's hand pulled me out of the room and re-sealed it. "Not a good idea to stay in there too long."

"That was a seed," I said still not believing what I'd seen.

"A very big one, and did you see what was behind it?" I shook my head 'no'. "An escape hatch."

"You think something is going to go for a space-walk?"

"I think we have a very big problem."

Just then my com sounded. I answered it. "Lang here."

"It's Tulla. Where are you?" she asked with a clear, calm voice.

I looked to Raph for ideas, but he just shrugged. "We're back near engineering. I think we found something."

"I'll bet you did," Tulla said, not trying to hide her sarcasm.

I put the com away. "She's ready to kill us."

"And now the Hagl know that we know this ship is the key to whatever their plan is. We'd better move fast." And he did. In the blink of an eye he was at the door, and in another blink he was heading down the hallway. It was like someone had sped up a video of him running. I ran after him.

When I found him he was at a control panel, like the ones I'd seen on the MaTeS, only bigger. His Guide's bookmark or interface was plugged into a data port on the front of the panel.

"Watch the door," he ordered; he'd lost all of his casual attitude.

I didn't argue but stood watching the hallway in both directions. I looked over at Raph, who was pulling wires out of the panel. "What are you doing?"

"Okay, if they can't get there, then they can't attack--right. So let's make sure they can't get there."

"What do you need me to do?" He looked at me with a confused expression. "Raph, I'm not an idiot. I can help."

It took him a while to answer, like he'd forgotten how to talk. "Okay, set all those instruments to full. That should be enough to blow the ship."

I started doing what he asked but then thought out loud. "If we blow up the ship, what happens to us?"

"Yeah...still sort of working on that."

"And what about Tulla? She's innocent. You can't just...." I didn't want to finish the sentence.

"One thing at a time. Okay?" I had to admire how Raph could put looming death to one side, so that he could blow himself up without being distracted. "Hit the blue button on the screen and then punch in 182-4-3."

I did what he said, and up came a countdown. We had about fifteen minutes to get off the ship. "Time to run?"

"Time to find Tulla," Raph told me as he grabbed up his Guide. "We have plenty of time so there is no need to worry. If nothing else I can open a portal to the Library and get us out of here. I just don't want to leave Tulla."

I hadn't realized that I was so tense. Raph's explanation helped. We ran out the door and toward the Bridge. I pulled out my com and called Tulla.

"Hey we're heading to the Bridge. Meet you there. Oh, and hurry."

We got there just as she did. I'm guessing she was on an upper deck looking for us. She was a quarter of the way around the sphere from us. "You two! Freeze, or I'll shoot!"

"Okay, but we just set the ship to blow in about ten minutes. So...," Raph said with his hands raised.

"You're bluffing!" Tulla shouted.

I shook my head. "Check it out if you want."

Raph added, "You can see the overload building on the engines' Reactor Conversion Flow panel."

Tulla moved around to a workstation and glanced down at it. "You two are insane!"

"No. We can get out of here without a problem," Raph told her.

"But we weren't going to leave you here. Tulla, we're not the bad guys here. What did they tell you?"

"That you two were spies!"

"Oh, come on," I said rolling my eyes. "Don't you see you're being played?"

"By you two, yeah, I see that!" Remember how I was saying that the Hagl soldiers didn't have that *move-and-I'll-shoot* look; Tulla did.

"Tulla, you saw those Hagl. You saw them change in front of you," Raph's voice was calm and level, "You saw it, it was real."

"I know what you're trying to do!"

"We're trying to save you," Raph looked genuinely upset as he said this. "Don't throw your life away. Please."

"We'll go with you as prisoners, but just get off this ship," I pleaded.

"Please," Raph added and I got the impression that he'd lost a lot of people. He'd said that his friends were dead; now I was wondering if that was his fault. Had he done something that caused them to die?

"No! I'm going to stop this! And you're going to help!" she shouted with real panic starting to show in her voice.

Raph closed his eyes and shook his head seemingly in defeat. I knew he had a plan, but it wasn't what I expected.

# *TIME TO DIE*

The Bridge was full of lights and sounds that were trying to tell anyone who would listen that the ship was in trouble. Raph and I were ignoring them; we were too focused on Tulla and her gun.

"I *will* shoot!" She looked panicked. I think the only thing keeping her together was the control she felt by being the one holding the gun.

"Don't care." Raph was ridiculously calm. "We'll be dead either way, but if you don't let us help you you'll be dead, too. Is that what you want?"

"I'll willingly die for the safety of Earth!" she called back.

"Tulla, dying here won't help Earth," I pleaded; I didn't want her to die. We had an out; she didn't. "Raph and I are already making sure that the Earth is safe. If you die, no one will know the truth about the Hagl, and Earth will still be off-guard."

She didn't lower her gun, but she lost some of that crazy-crazy look. Just then the five-minute warning went off. "It's too late. It takes five minutes to get to the shuttle and run through the disengagement protocols."

"What about the MaTeS?" I had to yell because of all the noise.

"If they were online, sure, but they're off line."

"Right then, it's the MaTeS," Raph said to me and grabbed my hand. The next second we were standing behind Tulla. Raph grabbed her with his other hand and then we were moving while standing still. We were in the hallway, and then at a corner, and then another and another. In seconds we were at the hangar.

"What the heck!" I yelled. Tulla looked as white as a sheet. Raph started running across the hangar and Tulla and I legged it after him.

"Van!" he called over his shoulder. "Remember how I told you that I could open a portal?"

"Yeah, to the Library!" Man he was fast, even in the cargo area's low gravity. He was already more than halfway there, and we'd only just started.

"I lied!" he shouted back at me. That got me running faster, Tulla too.

I reached the MaTeS just after him. Tulla was weighted down by her armour so she was pulling up the rear. "You *what*! How could you lie about something like *that?*!"

Raph was already messing with the hatch he'd opened on the other MaTeS to get it started. "I didn't want to worry you."

"*Thanks*! Anything I can do to help us *not* die?" I said literally jumping on the surface of the MaTeS.

"I think this'll work." Raph twisted up onto the platform with me. Tulla reached us just as he announced, "Get on, or stay here!"

Tulla dived at the platform just as Raph stabbed the 'on' button. Tulla hit the platform, but not the one in the *Pride* or the *Adventure*. We were back on the Hagl's ship. She was on her feet almost as soon as she hit the ground. "Where are we?"

"Not again!" Raph raged at the controls and whipped around the upright to access the panel again.

"We're on the Hagl ship. The one we told you about," I said while Raph poked at the controls.

"I thought we were going to the *Adventure*," she asked raising her gun and looking around. Just then the whole ship rocked. I knew without asking what had happened. The *Pride* had just blown up. I couldn't help but think, *what a waste*. All that information about far-distant space gone for good.

"That was fast," Raph said looking up and around. "I think I might have miscalculated."

"Shut up," Tulla barked as the shaking subsided. She had *that* look again, but at least the gun was pointing away from us this time. "How did we end up here?"

"Raph is the worst driver this side of...." I was trying to think of some star system that sounded far away, but settled for, "eternity."

"A mathematical impossibility," Raph said looking back down at the controls. "Tulla, who told you we were spies?"

"My commander," she said and then looked over at Raph and me. "Thought you said that you two were Specials?"

"We're more special than specials?" I said, and Raph laughed.

"You lied to me?"

"Yes," I said hoping that her gun didn't turn our way again. "Yes we did, but that's only because truth is weirder than believable."

"Are you lying to me now?" she asked and I shook my head. "Prove it."

I took a deep breath. "I'm from the 21$^{st}$ century, Earth's 21$^{st}$, that is, not Mars or Frog Star Beta or somewhere. Raph is from an extradimensional place called the Library. He sort of was trying to get me home, and we ended up in all this."

"You're right. That's not something to be believed," Tulla said, but this time with something like a smile. It vanished almost immediately. It took me a second longer to register that something was coming towards us.

"Tulla!" I hissed. "Hide!"

She stood her ground as Raph and I leapt to our hiding place behind the short wall. The *something* turned out to be four humans. The General was in the lead, talking to the person next to her. "We can't lose the other one. Get over there and make sure they don't get there before we do."

"Commander, sir?" Tulla asked not even trying to hide her shock.

"Oh Tulla, why did you have to come here? There must be Order," her commander said. "Where are your friends? On the *Adventure*, no doubt. Well, we'll find them, and Order them, too."

He drew his gun and shot Tulla in the chest. She never even tried to defend herself. I watched her fall like a ragdoll off the MaTeS platform. They didn't even look to see where she fell. Instead the General, Tulla's commander, and the two other soldiers stepped on the platform and vanished.

"Tulla!" I screamed as soon as they were gone. She was on the other side of the platform. I jumped over it in two leaps. Kneeling down next to her I said through the tears that clouded my eyes, "Just stay with me. We'll get you help."

Raph was standing next to me, his hand on my shoulder. "Van...she can't hear you, she's dead."

"She can't be," I cried. "She can hear me, she's just knocked out. She has armour on. It protected her!"

"Not from point blank. The amour can't disperse that amount of energy from that close." His voice was soft and kind, and I hated it.

"Is this what travelling with you is like? Just a trail of bodies with no one but you left standing! How long is it until I'm the one lying on the floor somewhere without anyone knowing what happened!" I yelled.

"Van, she was a soldier. That's what they do. They die, maybe not all of them, but lots of them," he said in that same stupid voice. "Now there are a lot of people who didn't sign up to shoot at others, who may die if we don't stop the *Adventure*. She was nice, but so are a lot of other people. Don't let them die because you're trying to save one person."

I looked up at Raph. He looked as calm as he sounded. I wondered out loud, "Are you even human anymore?"

I couldn't believe what he said and did. He shrugged. "I don't think so. I think this reality needs me to be something else. When will it be you on the floor? When you stop running after the monsters and give up."

Standing up I looked him in the eye. "You're right. You're not human."

"But I still care," he said softly. "Now are we going to save the Earth?"

I hated him at that moment, more than I have ever hated anyone. I hated him because he was right. "Yes."

# THE SEED OF DOOM

Instead of going to the *Adventure* and confronting the General (or the *murdering scum* as I'd started to think of her) we went to find information. Green mist was everywhere. Out in the main corridors it laid on the ground like ghost turf. Raph walked in front of me waving his Guide. It caused the dead calm of the mist to suddenly come alive in patterns of swirls. We knew that this would at least confuse the Hagl, if not blind them to us.

It seemed to take forever to get to where we were going. I watched Raph fanning and creeping, and wondered if I even liked him. We'd been running and trying not to die so much that I hadn't stopped to think about it. Not really.

I remembered what he was like in school. He was friends with my best friend Leonard. We used to call Len, Smudge, because he always had pencil or ink on the side of his hand. Smudge thought Raph was cool. I met him at a few parties, and out sometimes. Back then, Raph was a bit of a loner. I mean he'd hang out with Smudge and the gang but was never really part of it. Smudge and the others were more like the core of our group. Raph and I were outliers. We were the ones who others liked but no one really counted on for a good time. So here is the problem: Raph and I should have known each other better. We shared friends and interests. We should have, but we didn't know each other. Does that mean that there was something about the guy that I didn't like? Am I seeing that now? Or are we a bit too much like each other to get on?

Before I came to an answer, we got to wherever we were heading. The place looked like it was hollowed out instead of built. There is this Australian wasp I read about that builds its nest with mud. The Nests look seriously freaky. That's what this looked like, only from the inside. I was hoping that there were no huge wasps in here. I didn't see any, but what I did see were mud-coloured strings that ran everywhere. It was like this part of the ship had been woven or spun.

Raph of course had his Guidebook out scanning the place. I walked over to one of the 'threads'. There were millions of them, and they all looked to be about as thick as my arm. I touched the one I'd walked up to. It felt slippery. I can't think of a better word for it. It wasn't slimy like pond scum or oil. It was more like what a magnet must feel like, if you were another magnet of the same polarity.

When I touched it, my head filled with all sorts of information. It was kind of like when Raph hacked my brain so that I could understand his Guide. Again my mind was flipping through information too fast to read. I could sort of see things and get an idea that there are pictures or diagrams but they might have been videos or even full-length cinema movies. But again, I couldn't take in anything other than a sort of drumbeat. It reminded me of the sort I'd heard in documentaries. War drums.

Pulling my hand away from the thread I saw that Raph had moved. His Guide was now 'plugged' into what I can only guess was a data port. It looked like a spot where the mud didn't lay evenly, but was folded over. His bookmark was tucked up into the fold. The expression on his face told me that my impression of the Hagl plan wasn't wrong. This was an attack.

His words about saving many instead of just saving one still rang in my ears. I hated him for being honest with me about that. There was no sympathy in him. Had he lost that with his friends?

"Did you find what you were looking for?" I asked him as he tucked his bookmark away.

He nodded and started to turn away but stopped. "You know, too, don't you?"

"They are going to war against Earth, right?"

"That's what I've worked out, too," Raph's face was grim, and he didn't look me in the eye as he said, "I'm sorry about being callous. Tulla seemed like a nice person."

I got even madder at him. How could he be nice when I wanted him to be rude? "I won't know."

"Van, when you're a Time Grafter people die around you. A lot of the time they die because they can't keep up. Sometimes, like with Tulla, they are just in the wrong place at the wrong time. There is nothing we could have done without exposing ourselves to the same fate. She died, but we can still save the Earth."

He was right. Damn it! "I still think you've forgotten what it's like to be human."

With something like sorrow or sadness he said, "I know."

We stood there in silence for a while not looking at each other. I still wasn't sure that I liked him, but at least he was being honest with me finally. I broke the silence by asking, "What did you find out."

"The *Adventure* is their back-up ship. The pod-thingy we saw was a seed. The pyramids are how they plan on planting the seed. They'll bore down with the drilling soil, and then drop the seed in."

I thought that sounded daft. "I don't get it. Who's ever heard of one plant taking over the world?"

"This is not just one plant. It's a city seed. It's all the material for an entire invasion force that will grow underground. It will even grow these ships." He said, waving his arm so as to invite me to look at the organic structure of the ship.

It almost made sense, but there was still one flaw in the plan. "Someone on Earth would notice a huge city growing under their feet."

"It won't be under their feet. It will be on Mars."

"Mars?" I said more than a little surprised. "Why Mars?"

Raph smiled in that sort of way that just made me want to punch him. "Who would notice it there?

It could grow for a decade and no one would have a glimmer of an idea that it existed. Then when the Hagl are ready, they'll launch their attack while Earth is largely undefended. Earth's main line of defence is out near Jupiter. It would take them a while to scramble to Earth."

The idea that we were talking about Earth losing a war in ten years that the Hagl were on the verge of winning now made my blood run cold. "How do we stop them?"

Raph shook his head, "I don't know. We can't warn Earth, the General will have already closed those doors. We could just blow up the *Adventure*," Raph must have seen my face darken because he continued with, "but that would cause other problems. Any ideas?"

I started thinking out loud. "If they are going to Mars then they must think Mars is safe."

"Actually, they're going to Earth. This ship will stop at Mars, but the *Adventure* will continue on after it drops the drilling soil and the seed. Eventually the ship will have an accident and will be lost. The loss of two ships will get Earth looking for structural or engineering faults. It will stall new ships being built."

I sighed. I knew Raph was trying to get into my head. He was trying to get me to think about something other than Tulla. It was working. "So Earth pauses its shipbuilding leaving the Hagl time to prepare. Okay so we need to warn Earth, stop the *Adventure*, *and* destroy the seed. Did I miss anything?"

"We also need to figure out why you brought us here," Raph added.

"What? Me?"

# HONESTY

Raph blamed me for us being here. But how, could I do that? He was driving. I was just the passenger. He looked at me like he was daring me to try lying. So instead of saying anything, I was planning on waiting him out. There was a sort of creepy silence building between us. It might have something to do with the room we were standing in. Honestly, it looked like someplace you'd expect to see a huge, human-sized slug.

Raph was about to say something, but there was a sound from somewhere far away. It sounded like someone noticed us. I think we knew what the other was thinking: *time to save the Earth, time to run!* And we did.

Raph had his Guide in hand as we ran. He was only half-looking as he was sliding his fingers over a page. I took point and checked to see if the coast was clear. I got to the first corner just as there was a whacking-big crunch and the whole ship shook. I was able to keep my feet under me, but panels and twig-like things fell into the passage.

I'd only just caught my balance when Raph came up next to me. "Okay. That's this ship sorted. It's visible, and if the *Adventure* doesn't fire...."

"They'll know something's up," I nodded. "So we just sit back and let them kill each other?"

"No, it's not going to be that easy."

I sighed. "Figured that."

"We need to get to the MaTeS fast," Raph said slamming his Guide shut.

We were close to the hall where the MaTeS was when an explosion erupted in the hallway. Fire ripped towards us and all we could do was dive to the floor. It ripped along the ceiling above us. It got real hot, real fast. Then the fire was gone, and I couldn't breathe. The hall became blindingly cold. Raph pushed me through a door next to us and slammed his fist on the 'close' button.

I was raking in huge lungfuls of air, but it wasn't helping much. Even though Raph was right next to me his voice sounded like it was coming from down a tunnel. He was saying, "Take it easy. There's not a load of air in here. Just try to relax."

Have you ever tried to relax while your lungs feel like they're on fire? I tried, and eventually the ringing in my ears quieted and my heart slowed to something slower than a rave beat.

While I was trying to get over my latest near-death experience, Raph was on his feet looking around. "What...what...?" was all I could say.

"What happened?" Raph asked and I nodded. "I'm guessing hull breach."

Just then there were a whole lot more explosions. You know in the movies when you see a spaceship get hit and everything shakes? Well, when the real thing happens, yeah everything shakes, but that's not all. There are these waves of pressure that pass and suck the air out of you. Then there is the ringing, like you're standing in the world's largest bell. Oh man, it all hurts. Raph came running over to me and yanked me to my feet.

There was a hissing sound that was getting louder. "Van, do you trust me?"

"No!" I had to shout, "Why?"

"I can get us out of here," He was looking out a portal at the *Adventure*. It was lighting up the space around us as it fired and fired. "But I'll need you to trust me!"

My ears were starting to ring again, and not from the hull's deep, unending tolling. From the first minute I was on this ship, I thought that it looked like a second grader had constructed it out of tongue depressors for a school crafts project. Now it was coming apart the same way. Something metallic-tasting dripped on my lips and as I wiped it away I saw it was blood from my nose. The hissing must be the room's atmosphere being sucked out into space. I saw that Raph was bleeding from the nose, too. "Okay! Get us out!"

Just as Raph grabbed my arm, there was the feeling like I was being turned inside-out. I figured that I was being launched into space. This was the end. This time it really was over.

Then there was an impossibly sweet, hopelessly massive, amount of air. I could breathe again, and it was wonderful. I fell to my knees, and stuffed my lungs with what they were craving. Raph was kneeling next to me doing the same.

When I was able to talk I said between my puffs, "Where are we?"

"On the...*Adventure*." Raph sounded as winded as me.

"H...ow?"

"I teleported us here," he said sitting on the floor.

"With a MaTeS? I didn't...didn't...ah?" My head was still swimming and my thoughts were not washing ashore.

"Sorry, I should have said before--but...you know how it can be."

I felt an idea break through the mist that still seemed to fill my head. "You can teleport?" Raph nodded. I remembered how we ran in the *Pride*. "That was you! You? You!"

Raph could see that I was about ready to murder him. "It wasn't all me; it was you, too."

"Don't try to pin this on me, you jerk!" I screamed and jumped him. I started swinging at him, but he was too fast. I kept missing, and then I felt a sort of vibration. It felt as normal as breathing. I focused, swung, and hit him for six. He fell backward. When he landed I saw he was laughing.

"What do you think you're playing at, stupid...?" I couldn't think of anything mean enough to call him so just said nothing.

"You did it. You warped reality," he laughed. "Nice hit by the way."

"You...jerk! How many times?" I howled. "How many times did we almost die, when you could have saved us!"

"Ah...." and then he had the nerve to think about it. He started counting on his fingers again. "Okay three times really, but there were a few other times that I could have gotten us out of trouble. Do they count?"

"What?" What kind of stupid question was that? Great! I'm stuck in space with, at worst a homicidal maniac, or at best a whack-job. "Yes! They count!"

"Okay Van, listen. I know it sounds like I could have gotten us out of every scrape but that's not how it works. We needed to be in those places at those times to find out what was going on."

He sounded so cool, so calm. This was not the guy I knew in school. "I have no idea who you are. You look like Raph and maybe you used to *be* Raph; but not anymore! You're someone who uses people as bait, and then forgets to reel them in. Tulla might still be alive if you'd just zapped us out of there! Instead, you left her to die!"

Something must have sunk in because Raph looked really-truly shocked. "You used to say that didn't you?"

"Say what!?" I yelled. I was so...damn annoyed, and there was no way I was going to be derailed now.

"So that means...oh man, I think I know who you are, but that is even worse."

I wiped the tears that had started to form in my eyes. At least I see now, and Raph was no longer looking cool; he looked as scared as me. He started pacing and muttering to himself. I could hear words like, Chronopleonasmos and Chronotsama occasionally, but they meant nothing to me. Either my link to the Guide cut out, or the translator couldn't make them any clearer.

I felt for the link. It was still there but when I thought about the word 'Chronotsama' it gave me nothing. I pulled the word apart. 'Chrono' I'd already worked out. So what does 'tsama' mean? The Guide told me that it is loosely translated as 'lie'. A time-lie? What's that?

As I was trying to work out what Raph was muttering, I realized that he might not have all the answers. Maybe he was telling the truth again. I mean, we are trying to save a planet, but did Tulla have to die for it?

"Okay." My voice was a lot calmer. "Sorry. You're not a total jerk-face. I was just really, *really* scared."

He looked over at me like he wasn't sure what he was seeing. "Why would you create extra time?"

"Me?" The question was so random.

"Well, not you exactly. I mean why would *one* create extra time?" he asked scratching his head.

"Because you'd want a bit more in case something happened." I was just talking; I had no idea what about.

Raph snapped his fingers. "Or to hide something. Okay, let's say there's something you want to hide. What if you wrapped it up in paper and then put it in a box?"

"Me?"

"You're the only other person in this conversation," Raph insisted, but I wasn't certain I was. He seemed to be talking and thinking enough for at least two people.

"I'd say that was more like a gift than hiding something."

Wide-eyed, Raph smiled. "Me too."

"Great." I smiled back, maybe a little less sincere than his, or a lot less, to be honest. "What does that mean?"

Raph gave me two thumbs up. "It means we're about to crack this problem wide open."

"How?" I asked, hoping that the answer wasn't, *I'll tell you later.*

"Okay first thing we need to do is...." but he never finished because just then the door to the room in which we stood slid open and there stood the General, Tulla's commander, and two guards with guns.

# CHANGE IN THE ENVIRONMENT

Raph and I raised our hands. "I'm getting really tired of this."

"Well then let us put you out of your misery. Guards, on my mark you will shoot them."

As the guards raised their guns, I could see that those little lights that Raph had pointed out before were now shining brightly. Raph said, "Okay, shoot if you'd like. But then you won't know where the bomb is until it's too late."

The General was smiling as she said, "Nothing gets on or off this ship without my knowing it."

Raph grinned. "We did."

"A few times," I added.

The General indicated to the guards to lower their weapons. She and the commander both looked concerned. "Tell me."

"You forgot the magic word." Raph was instantly at his most annoying.

"Tell me," the General said slowly and quietly, "or I'll shoot the spare."

She was pointing at me as Raph said, "Didn't your mother teach you that you'll get more with honey than vinegar?"

"What has bee excrement to do with any of this?" the commander asked. He looked genuinely confused.

Raph's plan worked. I would guess that just about every human knew what that expression meant, but not an alien.

I lunged at the commander. The guard opened fire and missed. I had aimed my punch at the commander's throat, or where it would be on a human. I hit the spot *hard*, and the commander stumbled backward. It lost its focus, and two seconds later it was back to its Hagl form.

Raph was moving, too. One second he was in front of the guards, the next he was behind the General. I didn't see what he did, but she screamed and stumbled forward. The guards panicked as she changed form, and by the time they stopped there wasn't a lot left of either Hagl.

"Listen," Raph said quickly to the man and woman with guns pointed at us. "There is no bomb, but there are more of these things on board. My name is Raph, that's Van. We're Special, and until now, undercover."

"But how do we...?" the female guard asked.

With a quick lift of his shirt, a gold shield was visible for just a second. "Get to the Bridge and guard it. Arrest anyone who looks like they're getting sick. Van and I will take care of the rest."

Both the guards were in shock so I helped them along. "Now!"

They ran one way and we went faster in the other. "We need to get to environment controls. I know where it is, but we have literally seconds. Can you get us there without problems?"

"How would I do that?" I asked, my feet pounding the floor in step with Raph's.

"Move!" Raph yelled at a group of people standing in the corridor. "Remember when we were here before, and no one else seemed to be? That was you.

Just focus on where we're going, and how if we don't get there in time, Earth will die."

I stressed and picked up the pace. Suddenly everyone faded away. Raph and I were the only ones left in the hall. As we ran, I felt this sort of freedom. It almost felt like I had wings. "This is amazing!"

"Say focused, if you don't everyone *will* die." Raph shouted. That killed my buzz. Then he started calling out directions. "Left. Right. Right again. Left and up. Here!" We skidded to a stop. "This is it."

Inside the room were lots of monitors, and two lab-techie-looking guys. Raph and I jumped them. One, my guy, was human. The other was Hagl, and tried pulling a gun. When Raph took him down, he made sure the Hagl didn't get back up.

"What is that?" the man screamed as he recovered from my blow.

"It's a Hagl," Raph said, pulling out his Guide and plugging it in. "We need to adjust the environment a bit. Make the *Adventure* less suitable for these folks."

The man came up and watched the levels on the screens start to change. "You won't be able to change the environment, at least not for long. We're having all sorts of problems with it. The oxygen mix is lower than it should be."

"I think you'll find the system is working fine now. In fact let's give everyone a bit more $O_2$, since they've been so deprived," Raph said.

"You mean that guy," I pointed to the floor were the Hagl laid, "was messing things up?"

"Again, got it in one," Raph said pulling his Guide's bookmarks out of data ports.

All around the room monitors started showing changes. Up flashed a warning. It read, "Unknown element. Use caution."

"What is that?" the man asked, pointing at the screen.

"That's a little something to make sure that the increase in oxygen is taken up more quickly," Raph said to the technician. "Now. Stay here. I've rigged it so that the environment will normalize in about an hour. Don't touch anything, and seal the door once we're gone. And I mean seal it, not a soul comes in here for an hour."

I reached down and grabbed the pistol the Hagl had tried to use and handed it to the man. "If they insist, use this on them."

"Good idea," Raph smiled. "Okay ready?" As I nodded, he asked the technician, "How long until we reach Mars?"

The man tapped a window on the monitor and up popped a countdown. "We have about six hours at this speed."

"Well, that's not a lot of time but I guess...," Raph started to say when all of a sudden the timer sped up; hours turned like seconds. Suddenly just over six hours dropped to just under a half hour. "Damn, they must have figured out that they are in trouble, and sped up. We need to run."

Before the man realized that Raph was being literal, we were out the door. I came up next to him. "Where are we going?"

"To the Bridge," Raph told me as he started to pull ahead of me again.

I tried to get us there without anyone getting in our way, but my head wasn't clear enough. I couldn't block out the fact that we were winning. At least it felt that way until we got to the Bridge. The two guards we'd sent ahead lay just outside the door. I stopped and checked them; both were still alive. They had only been stunned.

"Now what?" I asked. "This is a bit of a Mexican standoff, isn't it?"

Raph agreed. "So we need something to tip the balance in our favour."

He pulled out his Guide and started typing something. Just then the tannoy announced in the General's voice: "Attention. This is General Bellentha. We are facing an invasion from a race of creatures called the Hagl. Special agents Raph and Van are scanning with a form of radiation that will only affect the Hagl. If someone near you becomes ill and-or collapses, restrain them. The Hagl are shape-shifters, and will revert back to their native forms. Security is to gather the Hagl and restrain them in the brig. These orders cannot be rescinded. As I said these aliens are shape-shifters, and will try to counteract these orders. Deadly force is authorized for defence only. Do your best, defend the Earth. End announcement."

I couldn't help but laugh. Raph stowed his Guide, "Well, they've been doing that to us for so long, let's see how they like it."

"Are we really scanning them?"

Raph shook his head. "No, but that's not something I want to tell the Hagl, is it? Really it's the oxygen that will make them sick."

A long list of ways to fight the Hagl were flying through my head, and oxygen was not included. "Why oxygen?"

"The Hagl are a plant-based life form. Remember how there was almost no oxygen on the ship? To them oxygen is a waste product."

"Will it be enough to kill the seed, too?"

Raph shook his head. "No, we still need to find it and get rid of it."

I thought I saw a problem in Raph's plan. He was good but I'd already seen that he wasn't perfect. "But then shouldn't we be looking for the seed?"

"We'll need to take the Bridge first. It can over-ride just about any plan I can think of except for adjusting the environment."

"But why not just admit that we changed the environment settings then?"

"You saw that guy in Environmental Control; would you count on him being able to defend it?"

I shook my head. "They'd fry him and replace him in a second."

"Van," Raph softened his voice, "I am still human. I do care about people. Just, I can't do it all the time."

"It's cool, Raph. Sorry about thinking you'd gone off the deep end."

Raph grinned. "Le peche?"

"You know, considering what we need to find, that joke is...bad." I was going to say in poor taste but then that would be an even worse joke. I think I was finally starting to understand Raph.

"Okay, you ready?" he asked letting his hand hover over the door's opening panel.

"Yeah," I said, and actually meant it.

He slapped the panel and the door slid open. The *Adventure*'s bridge was like the one in the *Pride*, only larger. There were about fifteen people in there. Five of them were Hagl. The rest where on top of them, trying to stop them from escaping. The Hagl were putting up a good fight. The ship's captain was pinned to the floor but was overpowering the two guards by hitting them with the hail from its head. Before anyone noticed us even enter, Raph was teleporting. He knocked out all five Hagl and was back. It took him something slightly longer than the blink of an eye. A second later he announced from the door to the confused room, "I'm Specials Agent Raph."

Out of his pocket he pulled a com. Now I know he didn't have one of those when he walked into the room. Did he just steal it? He spoke into the com, "Security, this is the Bridge. We have five Hagl to lock up."

After he tucked the com back in his pocket he walked in and around the twisting platform like he owned the place. "You," he pointed at a man who was wearing a helmet with a long visor, "Send guards to defend Environmental Control. Also I need a full E. M. scan of this ship," he said to a woman almost directly over top of him. Her helmet had a screen covering one of her eyes. He then pointed at another man with a similar screen folded down. "You help her. We're looking for a very unique form of radiation."

There were 'yes sirs' shouted out from three different directions.

There was a moment of silence before a woman next to me said, "Agent Raph, there is a shuttle powering up in Launch Hold 3."

"Stop it," Raph ordered, but the woman was already shaking her head.

"I can't retract its authorizations. I'm locked out."

Raph turned to me. "It's the launch bay next to--"

"The one we first arrived in. I'm on it." And I ran. Everyone vanished as I moved. I was not as fast as Raph, but I might just be fast enough.

# *FALLING TO MARS*

I knew the ship was big, but the way I was moving I swear it was shrinking. The corridors were blurring as I ran, and yet I could still make the corners as well as if I was walking.

It felt amazing to run like this, but my goal was directly ahead. I slowed down and that's when I saw him; there was a passenger still running for the open hatch. I passed him like he was standing still. I mean not literally, but I overtook him pretty quickly. And then I punched him. He hit the ground with a 'ker-thawp' and didn't get up. I think I still had some of that vibration energy around me, because I've never hit that hard. I'm more of a talk-and-runner than a stand-and-fighter.

There were four identical shuttles in the hangar. They looked like silver bricks with small tank track feet attached to landing-gear legs. On top was a motor that took up most of the roof; small ones poked out of the crafts' eight corners. Each shuttle had large sliding doors on their left and right sides. To the rear of the doors were mechanical arms. They were like you might see on a deep sea mini-sub only bigger. Almost as soon as I came into view one of the shuttles fired up its thrusters. As it began to pivot I saw it was carrying two pyramid-shaped crates. As it started forward towards the way out its hatches began to close. With one burst of speed, I was on board. The inside of the shuttle was sort of like a huge helicopter. Both wide exterior doors were now shut. The space or room I was in was maybe five-by-five metres. An equally large room was to my right on the other side of a thick, glass-like wall. Its hatch was made of the same clear material and was about the same size as the outside doors. It stood open. As I looked quickly around the room I saw the whole back wall could open, like on a cargo plane. At the centre of the backroom was the Seed. It looked just like the one from the *Pride*, but it was secured with some sort of webbing. The part that worried me was the green mist flowing from it.

Unlike the big ships, this shuttle's pilot sat up front, and I was on him in a flash. He first hit a button and the shuttle shot out of the *Adventure* into open space. Then he shifted into an it. It hit me *hard*! The Hagl, now in its rotting-stick-figure-and-snowball-head form, had twig-like fingers that were as sharp as spears. I didn't want to get sliced by them. I was trying to get a few solid shots in but the thing was fast.

I wished I wasn't fighting for my life, because I think I'd have liked the view. Outside, Mars looked like a red version of Earth as seen from the Moon; inside it was all fists and claws. At least the shuttle had artificial gravity so I was trying not to die in only two dimensions. I quickly worked out that it was a lot better at fighting than me. I did my best by kicking and punching at it, and then I saw a way I might win this.

I dived for the hatch controls. I was hoping the Hagl would think I was going to try to space us. It blocked me, but the thing is that the link between me and Raph's Guide was still open. I could feel the information there, just beyond my thoughts. It answered my question: How is the hull cooled and heated? The answer was, by using an oxygen and nitrogen exchange system. So when the Hagl blocked me from the hatch controls it left open a path to the emergency oxygen release valve. I grabbed it and pulled.

Something between a liquid and a gas hit the Hagl full in his snowy-storm head. A second later, it fell over seemingly dead. I wasn't about to take any chances. I pushed the body into the back of the shuttle. After figuring out how to seal the glass-like door dividing the two halves, I pressed the back hatch release. The interior wall and door fogged as the rear airlock opened. I breathed a sigh of relief as I watched the Hagl disappear into space.

My reprieve from death only lasted a few seconds, because out the front window was a very large red and green planet approaching. I panicked. I didn't know how to fly a spaceship and I had only seconds to learn. To add a bit more tension to the situation, some sort of alarm started screeching.

I tried to think, but the noise was making my brains scramble. Finally I pulled my eyes away from the really, *really* big planet of Mars. Honestly it was as red as...RED! I started looking for anything red and pushed it. There were all sorts of sounds now.

Mars no longer looked smooth. I could now see mountains and valleys. It wasn't *all* red, just mostly red. This was it. I was going to die, and I thought how no one will ever know what happened. They would just think I disappeared on the way to a friend's house. But then I thought H*ey, I'm two-hundred-and-a-bit-years-old*. That's older than I ever expected, and I'm going out saving a planet. That's pretty chill.

I smiled and then was thrown backward. The shuttle stopped heading straight for the ground, it had turned sharply. I got to my feet and looked out the front screen. The shuttle was now flying parallel to the ground. I think I'd feel a lot more relaxed if the alarms weren't still going off.

The shuttle dodged and weaved between mountains until I could see a large strip of green. Maybe I shouldn't be smiling; maybe I should keep pressing red things. I jammed my fingers at anything I could until I read *Auto-Pilot*. It was engaged. I slid the blue switch from the up position to the down position. And that got a response from the ship. The thrusters cut out and the shuttle sailed like a brick. In other words it fell out of the sky. I was flipped around like I was inside a tumble dryer before the shuttle stabilized.

When I recovered from being bounced off the floor, the ceiling and the walls, I ran for the centre hatch. In the back, the Seed was hissing loudly. That's when the world split. I don't mean that Mars cracked open and I flew through. What happened was this: I watched the future turn to history. It went off in two different directions. One history showed the Hagl successfully invading Mars. The other showed Earth with no neighbours. The first future history did not show the Hagl attacking Earth, but living next door and being a rival in this region. It changed us. It made humanity paranoid and more aggressive. The second history showed humanity repeatedly reaching out further and further until we were driven or pulled back, and then expanding again.

Both future histories showed humanity being very human. The one with the Hagl's colonizing Mars exposed a side of humanity that we have struggled to control for two thousand years. It was angry and hateful. On the other hand, the second one showed a side that we have struggled with for far longer. It showed pride and self-importance to the point of arrogance.

Neither future was all that great. Both depended on what I would do with the Seed. The choice between these histories was mine. I was about to determine the future of all humanity. Could I? Why should I be the one who decides? What right do I have to do it?

I opened the back hatch and watched Mars race by just outside. And then I understood. I had the right to choose because I was here; I made it to this point. If I'd walked on the other side of the pavement to Smudge's house or died on Mars or the Hagl ship or the *Pride* or the *Adventure*, I wouldn't be here. But I *was* here and I had the chance to make a choice. I could stop the Hagl's plans. Wait! *Was* it theirs?

That's when I felt something else. There was a future history behind the Hagl's plan. I couldn't make it out clearly. Whatever it was, it was manipulating all of this. It was like there was a hand trying to change the future by pushing the Hagl and humans into conflict. I wasn't able to focus on it for more than an instant, but I had seen it. It didn't fill me with a very nice feeling.

If whatever that hand was, was trying to create a history where the Seed planted the Hagl here, then I was going to do the opposite. I closed the hatch and ran to the shuttle's controls. I *needed* to understand how to stop from crashing.

The information came to me as clear as if I was watching a YouTube video. I could freeze the Seed by adjusting the backroom's atmosphere. I did it, and then started following the instructions on how to land. And just like what always seems to happen with those videos, real life was different. The landing thrusters weren't firing. I was going to have to 'belly-flop' the shuttle.

I watched the ground get closer and closer, and then I heard and felt it. The shuttle hit the ground like a stone skipping over water. The whole shuttle wrenched around so it was sliding sideways. I could hear metal shredding just a metre below my feet. Then something caught and the ship cartwheeled. I was thrown and pinned to the wall like I was on a funfair ride, and I hated it. The front screen started to crack and the side hatches were denting in. I had the feeling that the shuttle was starting to become a ball instead of a cube. Finally with one big flip the crafted stopped rolling and spinning.

It was still sliding backward and on its side but a lot slower. I pulled myself out of the spot where I had been pinned and slid down the floor to the wall. I needed a plan. What was left of the controls were too far above to reach. As I tried, I noticed out the front screen that a scar from the crash was growing. Rock and ground were falling into a deepening chasm. It was like watching sand pass through a sieve. It was like the ground was melting. Melting? Oh no! Where was the soil acid?

I had been too mesmerized by the gorge opening further and further to notice that the upper side of the shuttle had started to disintegrate. I could actually smell the drilling soil before I saw it. A dozen holes had opened from above, and brown sand-like powder was pouring in. It was eating the side I was standing on. I panicked. I had to get out of here before I was either crushed by the shuttle collapsing down onto itself, burned by the acid, or smeared across Mars' surface.

Quickly and carefully I moved over to the floor side of the shuttle. There was a bottom hatch within reach. It wasn't buckling yet. I tried turning its manual release. I twisted as hard as I could; nothing happened. I punched it and hurt my hand. There wasn't a lot of the shuttle left; maybe I could jump. How fast was I going? It was hard to tell. I could jump and then *run*. Just then what was left of the shuttle groaned and twisted. I was thrown as part of it collapsed. The whole roof pulled away and the craft slowly started to tumble down over itself. It was literally now or never. I jumped!

# HIT AND RUN

Just as my feet were about to land, I felt the vibration start. It was like I was in a cartoon. I was slipping along the surface of Mars like it was a waterslide. It was literally the funnest thing I'd ever done. But I enjoyed it a bit too long. The atmosphere was really thin, and I started having problems breathing. Off in the distance I could see the shock of vegetation that was Mars' Green Belt. I ran for it.

Oh man, running felt good. I could breathe okay again. It was like any problem I'd ever had was far away. I ran for the Green Belt. I didn't really want to, but I had no idea how long I could run for. When I had to stop, I wanted to be somewhere I could catch my breath.

By the time I got close to the vegetation I was glad I had started in this direction. I was getting fatigued. I noticed for the first time that there was a barrier, or limit to my running. The closer I got to that barrier the worse the fatigue got. By the time I got to the Green Belt I wasn't breathing hard, but it felt good to stop. The air was fresh and clean. I hadn't noticed onboard the ships that most of the time the air had a stale, metallic smell. It was the sort of air that lacked a life of its own.

"Okay, now what?" I said out loud. I had been in such a rush to get here that I never stopped to think about what to do after that. I figured that my best bet was to head towards a MaTeS. If someone else was going to come down here, I'd bet that it would be that way and not the way I did.

I started jogging through the plants, calling out for anyone who might be around. It was grace more than anything that led me in the right direction. Maybe ten minutes later I found a MaTeS pad in a clearing of what looked like two-and-a-half-metre-tall broccoli plants. I was hungry enough to break off a crown and start chewing on it. It tasted a bit weird, but mostly like broccoli.

Now that I found the MaTeS there was nothing else to do but sit around and wait. I went to pull my phone out and then remembered it was dead. I looked up. Straight over my head was one of the fake suns. Down here it felt warm, like an early summer day. I could almost convince myself I was back on Earth, but then I'd look up and the illusion vanished. The fake sun was lighting up a blue-black sky. There wasn't enough water vapour in the atmosphere to make it look like the Earth's sky. Down close to the horizon I could see another sun. I turned around and spotted a third one. They created a sort of light-band overhead. When I looked off to the sides the light faded. It was a weird idea that someone would want to grow plants on another planet. Growing them in space I guess I could understand. There is a lot of space in space, but on a planet would mean having to deal with all sorts of problems. Just getting it off the ground for starters would take a lot of energy. Then I thought about the MaTeS and MaTting it up. That would work. But then if MaTeS could move crops, why was the Hagl's plan to drop the seed.

Even though I was sure that this what? Case? was solved there were still a lot of things that didn't add up. I still didn't get why Earth was farming Mars to start with. I didn't understand why the Hagl even wanted to attack Earth. From what I could understand they hardly even knew where the Earth was. And yet they seemed scared of Earth, or humans. It sort of felt like the time when this girl told me that her boyfriend was going to beat me up because she thought I liked her. She was totally wrong, but I still had to watch my back for a couple of days. The thought was so random, that maybe there was something to it. Maybe the Hagl, in all their creepiness, were just reacting to some misunderstanding, or...ah man! I just remembered that other future, the one with the hand.

My head was buzzing with ideas. For the first time I felt really trapped. I jumped up on the MaTeS' platform and started really looking at how it worked. I was decent at understanding technology, and I had a cheat. Moving my finger from icon to icon I learned from my link to Raph's Guide how the machine worked. It took about twenty minutes to get to the point where I was ready to try to use it when an alarm started to sound from the controls. "Incoming transmission. Please clear the pad--Incoming transmission. Please clear the pad."

The alarm kept sounding until I stepped off the platform. From the centre of the platform a transparent, blue dome grew from nothing to fill the space. It was like someone was blowing a bubble. Then four figures appeared, blurry at first. The bubble vanished, maybe popped, and there was Raph with three crew members.

Raph stepped down first. "Quite a landing. Was there anything left of the ship?"

I sighed; we were back to bantering. No doubt something went wrong on the ship and he was afraid I'd blow his lie. "A bit. You here to pick it up or me?"

"If that's an 'or' question then the answer is the Seed. If it is an 'and' question then it is the Seed and you."

Shaking my head I pointed back the way I came. "It's over there somewhere."

Raph and I watched the three crew members follow the trail of broken stalks I'd left on my way here. Once they were out of sight I asked, "Did we do it?"

"Did we stop the Hagl's plan to implant themselves on Mars? I think so," Raph nodded.

He was answering only the question I asked, not the question I meant. "Did we stop the plot? I mean there is something else at work here, isn't there?"

Raph glanced over in my direction as he started walking in the opposite direction from where the crew members headed. "Meaning what?"

"Come on Raph; you know that the Hagl had to be put up to this. I mean, they hardly even know about Earth."

"And yet they had people all the way up to Earth Governance in on this," Raph said as we entered the vegetation.

"I don't know. It just feels like something really big is missing. Don't you feel it?" I said following him.

Raph did not push plants out of the way but carefully walked around them. Was he trying to make a discreet exit? "I think you're right. While I was pretending to be in the Specials I got the impression that there were a lot, I mean like huge, gaps in the *Pride*'s story."

"Didn't anyone else notice?" I asked stepping as carefully as Raph.

"No. Most of the mission information was doled out on a need-to-know basis."

I got it. "And the Hagl were deciding on who needed to know."

"Got it in one," Raph said and then stopped. "We're here."

I looked around. I had no idea where *here* was. I knew from the crop that we were not where we had first arrived nor were we near the first MaTeS we saw. "We're where?"

"Just in front of me is the Portal," Raph told me stepping to one side.

I saw nothing in front of me or him. "You sure? None of this looks familiar."

"The Portal moved to find us, and right now it is directly in front of you. Take three steps forward and you'll be inside the Library."

His voice was level, but I could tell he was hiding something. "What if I don't walk forward?"

"You'll die," Raph said flatly, and that got my attention. "I don't mean now, I mean eventually."

"Won't I die anyway?" I asked trying not to croak like a frog as I said it.

Raph shrugged. "I really have no idea. I'm older than I can count and yet still going. You might be the same."

"Will I be able to go home?" I asked even though I sort of knew the answer.

"No."

"Okay." I hoped I didn't sound as homesick as I suddenly felt.

"Van, you were chosen by the Library. There are Pivot-points all over the universe. Ones like the one you encountered when you had to decide what to do about the Hagl." How did he know about that? I was about to interrupt but then I changed my mind. I wanted to hear him out. "Those points decide the path the future will take. But there are other points, moments that access something deeper. Those thin parts I told you about before. You came out of one of those points. The Library can't put you back there. It's not safe to access it again."

"How do you know about the decision I had to make?"

Raph smiled. "Would you believe me if I said that it showed up in the Guide?"

"Maybe, but that's only half an answer."

"It was the reason I sent you ahead," Raph admitted. "I could feel the point coming, and one of us would have to make that call. You're more...attached to humanity than I am. The decision would be clearer for you."

I shook my head; he was lying. "You are so full of it. Okay, so what happens if I step into the Library?"

"No idea."

"You are *such* a jerk. Fine! Don't tell me," and I walked forward.

# BACK TO BASICS

The Library can take your breath away. I think it is the first place I've ever been that shouldn't feel as big as it does. That first moment you step in you can feel how endless it is. The second thing I felt was a sudden feeling that I was home. It was a sort of love at first sight. Only it wasn't the first time I'd seen this place and it wasn't really love. It was more like knowing that life is going to become really exciting. That's it! It was like passing through the gates to your own personal theme park.

Raph was right behind me. "Right, well you know the place, and so go ahead and explore."

"What about you?" I wondered aloud.

Raph sighed; he suddenly looked a lot older. "Me? I was planning on disappearing into the stacks for the rest of eternity, but I guess I'll have wait on that. I've got some calculations to do anyway."

"Raph, what about the Hagl, and the something that led them to Earth?" I wasn't sure he was listening, he looked so distant.

Eventually he answered me, "That's a question for another day. For now don't worry about it."

"You said that leaving me in the Library would have been dangerous. You said it didn't know me."

"I lied." Raph looked frustrated, like I was keeping him awake. "Okay, come on. I'm hungry. We'll talk in the café."

I followed him out of the Grand Central–like clearing and into the stacks of books. We weaved our way along for a few minutes until we came to an enclosed sort of building, or at least the front wall of one. It was massive, at least ten metres tall and wide, and made out of stone and books. Over the four metre tall door, carved into stone, was a single word, Café.

Inside the Gothic façade was a stupidly long, gothic, retro-cool, coffee shop. On the left side was a white, stone wall that reached as tall as the front wall. Along it ran café glass cases of food. The right side of the room was dominated by five stained glass windows. Each window was of an element. They were labelled Time, Water, Earth, Fire, and Air. At the end of the long room were shelves of books. They reached up to the top of the wall, and then up even further still. There was no ceiling to the café. The walls held up a metal walkway, and from there the Library continued. Scattered around the room were dozens of tables and chairs.

Raph paused at the entry and took in what he saw. "Hmm, this is all new."

"Is there a reason why the Library has a coffee shop that looks more like a cathedral?" I asked still looking around.

Raph was already picking a few sandwiches out of a glass case. "The Library knows I really like food. It didn't used to look like this. Everything in the Library tends to change."

"That's got to get confusing," I said joining him at the cases. I pulled out a pudding.

"Not really. It's not like the real universe, it just sort of feels nice. It's like moving the furniture around in your room."

That started him on telling me some basics about the Library and how he found it. He told me about the Librarian and the Information System that sounded like the woman from the grocery store ads. He was explaining about portals when I interrupted him.

"Raph," I said between spoonfuls of pudding, "We need to find out what happened to bring the Hagl to Earth."

He shook his head. "No. That's not our job. Our job is to be there for the Pivot-points and make sure a decision is made."

"Those people need us still," I insisted.

"What? To fight every battle for them? They can fight that one. We gave them a level pitch, they'll need to do the rest. What we really need to do is understand what you are."

That was a random change of topics. "Me? I get the impression that I'm something like what you are. So maybe the question should be, what are you?"

Raph shrugged. "No idea. I thought I was unique, but you seem to be evidence to the...you know, contrary. I got some interesting readings from you. Would you like to know what I learned?"

"Yes, duh."

"Okay, first off when you run you sort of affect the interface of time and space."

"Affect the interface?" I asked. "What does that mean?"

"Normally time and space lock together like gears." Raph bent his fingers and interwove his knuckles. As he turned his hands they slotted in between one another, working together. "When you run, time and space don't exactly meet up, or at least they don't lock together. You have the ability to separate them." He pulled his hands apart and turned them independently. "See? No interaction. It's like a form of linear time travel."

"Is that like what you can do?"

"No," Raph admitted. "I can step out of time, move in space, and then step back into time. It's fundamentally different."

"But it still works similarly?" I set my empty bowl aside and got up. I hadn't realized how hungry I was.

"Yeah," Raph said as he chewed. "That's the interesting part. The abilities are related."

I pulled out two sandwiches like Raph had, and noticed that the two that he had taken had somehow been replaced. "Are there other's like us?"

"No idea," Raph said leaning back and looking up into the Library. "I guess we could look for others."

"Is there space for others? I mean are there...you know, rooms?" I sat back down again, and now that there was something in my stomach, I was slipping into a food coma.

"The last time I was here," Raph waved his arms around at the café, "It was a small Parisian establishment with three tables and a vintage jukebox. The Library adapts. We have Pods. They're places to rest and heal. And as far as I can tell we have an infinite number of them."

"The Pods sound interesting. I could use some of both. I don't think I've ever been so bruised. But you keep saying *we*. I don't know if I'm interested in being part of a '*we*'. When I got up this morning, I was planning on hanging with Smudge. Now I've been on Mars, two--no three spaceships, flown a shuttle," Raph started to smile, "Okay, I crashed a shuttle. I've been attacked more times than I can count, and been told there is no way home. Sure some of it was cool, but a lot of it was just plain scary. Raph...." I couldn't finish the sentence.

He looked like he understood. "Yeah, it takes a while for it to settle in. It's cool, and by the way you've been at it for something like two days. *This morning* was a long time ago."

No wonder why I was so hungry. I got another sandwich. We finished eating and Raph showed me to a Pod. Oh man, they are cool. After that I walked around the Library. It was really, really quiet, but in

the silence I thought I heard something. At first it was only something like the idea of a sound. As I followed it, I was able to actually hear it. It was the sound of birds singing. At the end of a short stack of shelves through a stone arch was a clearing.

Trees with apple blossoms swayed gently in a light breeze. Near the middle of the clearing was a small hill. Long grass covered it, rippling like water. There was no ceiling in here, just blue skies with puffy clouds. The sounds of birdsong were even louder now. It was a perfect spring day. The sort of day you only read about in storybooks. To be honest I wouldn't have been surprised to meet a talking rabbit.

First off, I'll admit that I felt a lot better after being in the Pod. That was incredible. It was like dreaming reality, but this was almost as good. There was actually a sun and sky above, or something that looked like them. I walked up to the top of the hill and lay down. The sun felt great. It seemed to warm me from the inside out, and I needed that. Closing my eyes I could almost be back home. I say almost because there was no sound of the city.

Home. Oh God. Somewhere, at sometime, my mom is wondering when I'm coming back. Dad will blame her if I never show up again. It'll kill them if I've just disappeared. Smudge, too. That'd be two friends gone in one summer. I can't think about that right now. Okay, so if I can't go back then what am I going to do? I need time. I need to get away from this...stuff. I need to get away from the creepy aliens, and the...death. Until today I'd never even seen a dead person, and now I've killed. I need to figure out if this is what I'm going to become?

I just wish I could go home and at least say goodbye. Tell mom that I love her; I don't think I said it enough. I must have fallen asleep at some point because I seem to remember a sort of dream. There was a light, and there was a person saying, "One by one they will arrive."

It took me a few seconds after I woke up to remember where I was. Then it took me a few minutes to stop grinning like, well something that grins a lot. It was real; for the first time I realized that it was all real. I was in the coolest place in the universe, well, *outside* the universe, really. I was on a hill, in a meadow, surrounded by a Library. Now *that's* cool! I stood up. I was ready to really explore, and that meant I should check in with Raph. Just in case there was somewhere I wasn't suppose to go, you know what I mean.

I left the meadow, and went back the way I came. I found Raph in Grand Central. He was working at a desk with a funky kind of graph.

"Hey!" I called, "I've been thinking."

"So have I." He turned and walked over to where I was standing, scooping up a leather backpack on the way.

"I thought I'd take a look...." I said as he pushed the backpack into my chest.

"Open it," he said and then returned to the desk.

I did. Inside was a book, my phone, something that looked like a phone case, and a wallet. "What's this?"

He didn't look up as he said, "I think I found something. The something is more like a non-something. It shouldn't exist, but it does. It's hard to pin down but the closest I can get you to it is either

Tokyo, 1842--or the floating city of New Sydney, 2301. Which one do you want?"

And this was just like him. I was getting ready to tell him I wanted to look around, and he's already pushing me out the door. Jerk! "Ah...actually I was thinking about looking around in here."

"You can't." Now he did look up. "Van, you're a Time Grafter now. You have a responsibility to the universe."

"Can't the universe wait a bit? I mean those two time-dates are what, five hundred years apart?"

He shook his head. "Sorry, it doesn't work like that."

I think he just makes up the rules as we go. "I thought the Library was outside all that. I mean can't we just pop-in anywhere, anytime."

Raph looked over at me shaking his head, "And now I finally understand how Johannes felt. Like I said, it doesn't work like that. You're right, things happen within time, and yeah, we're outside it. But we need to be there for the lead-up. That means there are only a few insertion points where we can access specific chronoevents. And that means you need to go."

I looked at the leather backpack. "Why not you? I mean you're loads better at this."

"I'm better because I've been out there more. So which one? Tokyo or New Sydney?" Raph said turning back towards the desk.

I could tell that he was lying, or at least leaving things out. I thought, *he's testing me, so I'll trick him.* "I don't know. Which one do you think I'll choose?"

"Tokyo."

The total...JERK! I mean that is the one I was going to choose, but only because I love the idea that I'd be able to speak Japanese like a native. "Okay why Tokyo?"

"So that you can speak English and be understood in Japanese."

JERK!!! I looked inside the backpack. "Fine, what's all this stuff?"

"First off, I packed your phone. I doubt it'll work, but I thought you might want to have something from home. Also it'll tether to your Guide, and it'll fit in the case. The book is *your* Guidebook. It's coded to you, and only you. Use it like...well, like a Guidebook, and try not to lose it. The wallet has access to funds in local currency. You won't be rich, but you should have enough. I like to call the phone holder 'A Just-in-Case'. It's for emergencies; don't use it unless you really, *really* need to." He turned to another desk and pressed something. The kiosk's window started to shine with a bright light. "Your portal is ready."

"Fine," I said as I stretched the case around my phone and stuffed it into my front pocket. Slinging the pack on my shoulder, I entered the kiosk. "You'd better have gotten it right this...time?" Wherever I was, it wasn't Tokyo in 1842.

# A NEW START

It wasn't what I expected, and yet it was what I was getting used to. The part I didn't anticipate was that I was in a very short alley. It emptied onto a street that looked like something out of a black-and-white movie. I turned around to see where I'd come from. It was a brick wall with a poster in English saying that Wuthering Heights starring Thomas Graham and Gretchen Akury with Jane Bridges as Emily were available for purchase. At least I think it was English, maybe my Guidebook was translating. No. If it worked like Raph's, I'd know the language, not see it translated. Okay so that was the unexpected part; what was just totally typical was that this was *not* Tokyo!

I looked around for more clues about where I was. The cars parked on the road suggested it was United States in the 1950s. Just then an old-fashioned, yellow, checkered cab drove by. I was standing next to a theatre. Hanging over its entrance was an awning with the word Felshen outlined in old-fashioned light bulbs. So New York City, 1950s, maybe near Broadway? Not Tokyo 1842!

I pulled out my Guidebook. I figured that it would tell me where I was. Wow! This was no normal book. All of a sudden there was information all around me. It came to me not only through my eyes, but also by my ears, nose, skin, and then some sense that I didn't even know I had.

The six sense was like how I imagined telepathy would be. Only it wasn't exactly like that. It was more like I had a tablet or phone bluetoothed right into my thoughts so that my thinking was like apps running in the background. I could flip apps and see or know information, graphs, and pictures. There were things like the air was mostly nitrogen, but had a higher level of zinc, sodium, nickel, and mercury than normal. There was also a high concentration of carbon dioxide and lead. The road surface was mostly local stone, with tar and other petrochemicals. The building in front of me was made of clay, fired at between 1200° and 2300° C.

I squeezed my eyes shut and shook my head, trying to clear it. It suddenly ached, like all of my synapses were firing at the same time. There was this blindingly bright light, a hum so low and so loud I thought it was going to deafen me, and cold so intense it made my teeth hurt. Slowly I cleared my head by closing off that new sense that I had developed. When I chanced a look at the still open Guidebook in my hand I saw that it had graphics, not too different from the desks in the Library. Still trying to keep my mind clear, I turned like I'd seen Raph do. The graphics changed. So the interface was 3D as well. It was like a video game that moved with you, only without a screen. That was cool.

Tucking the Guide back in my pack, I looked around for someone to ask where I was. A man with a long trench coat and black hat was passing. "Excuse me, sir?"

"What?" Something about my style caused him to look at me funny. His face, his eyes were searching.

"Could you tell me where I am?" I asked, sounding a bit more like a tourist than an explorer.

"This is 45th. That's Avenue of the Americas or 6th and," he pointed in the opposite direction, "7th is that way."

"Thanks." That settles it. Avenue of the Americas, the intersection of two numbered roads, this has to be New York City. "Oh, what year is it?"

The man was already past and I don't think he heard me. If he did, he was ignoring me; probably because I sounded like a nutter. I pulled my Guide out again, but before I opened it I concentrated on one thing. *Show me something useful*, I told it, or I should say thought-at-it. I opened the book. It was completely blank except for three typed lines.

>> Estimated Population: New York City – 1958 – 3,934,192.
>> Actual Humanoid Heartbeats within 5 Boroughs: 5,216,012
>> Actual Animated Humanoids within 5 Boroughs: 5, 216,023

I closed the book, feeling like the bottom of my stomach just fell out. I was in 1958. I understood that. I was pretty sure that 'animated' meant moving and not drawn like in the cartoons. The part I was having problems understanding was that there are eleven people walking around without a heartbeat. Raph had sent me out to look for something that was wrong. I think I might have found it.

I needed to think about what I'd just read and work out some kind of plan, so I started walking towards 7th Avenue. It turns out that I was walking in the wrong direction. I worked that out by the sound of someone screaming. In response I twisted around and ran back.

The woman was screaming like she was in a cheesy horror movie. Okay maybe she thought she was on stage or something. Her hands were up by her face as she screamed, then she took a breath, and then screamed again. It sounded like a stage scream; it sounded fake. The reaction might have sounded unbelievable but the dead body at her feet was very real.

I got a better look as the woman was moved away. The body was the guy I'd just talked to. He was laying there face down. Actually, he looked frozen, almost like he was planking. I moved around him and saw the side of his face. It was as if he'd been turned to plastic. His face now resembled a dropped egg, but unlike an egg there was nothing leaking out of it.

As others gathered around I was pushed aside by a police man. He quickly pulled off his trench coat and crouched down. I opened my Guidebook to take a scan. The first line read:

>> Killing pattern similar to that of the Hollowing.

After covering the top half of the man, he looked up at me, "I think you've got some explaining to do boy-o."

**To Be Continued...**

# EPILOGUE

Somewhere that is not in our universe, five dark creatures drift in a circle looking in at the scene of the dead man on the New York City street. One of these monsters of darkness declares, "Order has failed. The Hagl have failed. Order is not acquired."

"What was the hand that turned fate and stopped Order from occurring?" another asked.

"One calling himself a Time Grafter," the first one responded.

"What is one?" a third asked.

"One is not us. One is alone, and without requirement. One acts as if it can change Order," the first announced.

If it were possible, the other four phantoms would have looked worried. A fourth monster asked, "They have set themselves against us?"

"But they are our kin," the third nightmare stated.

"No," the first said almost showing an emotion, "they have turned their backs on the darkness to face the light. They will not follow Order."

"The Hollowing are in place," another of the nightmares stated.

The fifth and last one said in an even colder and dryer voice than the others, "We shall darken these paler copies of their greater predecessors. We shall tear them from the light."

# Inside a Nightmare
## Foundations: Book Two

The stage was empty but for a dead body lying on it. Sally and I ran over to it. Just as I guessed: it was Helen. Her body was hollowed out, just like the others. Crouching down, I gently tapped her skin with the back of my fingernail. It was hard, just like the others.

"It looks like she's been turned into a mother-of-pearl doll," Sally said, sitting back on her heels next to me.

I wanted to scan the body with my Guide, but once again I was reminded that I'd lost it. Helen's dead, plastic body also reminded me that I had no idea how to figure out what was going on without my Guide. The worst part was that I couldn't even get a message to Raph that there was trouble. I was on my own. Totally on my own, with no way to get back to the Library, and the dead were piling up.

# About the Authors:

### Written by: PG Somerset

PG Somerset lives in the seaside town of Glastonbury Beach, Delaware, with his cats who often try to help him write. He is the creator of the Time Grafters, an idea born out of a love for travel and learning.

### Cover art and plates by: K. Sparrow

Sparrow is a highly established graphic designer who has worked for major international corporations. His award winning artwork has been featured in traditional print and digital media.

**The more time we have, the more time has us. - PGS**